Also by Olivia Gaines

Modern Mail Order Brides
On A Rainy Night in Georgia
Buckeye and the Babe
The Tennessee Mountain Man
Bleu, Grass, Bourbon

Serenity Series
Welcome to Serenity
Holden
Farmer Takes A Wife

Slice of Life
Friends with Benefits

Slivers of Love
The Cost to Play
Thursdays in Savannah

The Blakemore Files

Being Mrs. Blakemore
Shopping with Mrs. Blakemore
Dancing with Mr. Blakemore
Cruising with the Blakemores
Dinner with the Blakemores
Loving the Czar
Being Mr. Blakemore
A Weekend with the Blakemores

The Davonshire Series
Courting Guinevere
Vanity's Pleasure

The Delgado Files
Killers

The Men of Endurance
A Walk Through Endurance
A Return to Endurance
An Endurance Christmas
A Walk Through Endurance

The Technicians
Blind Luck

The Value of A Man
My Mail Order Wife

A Weekend with the Cromwells
Cutting it Close

The Zelda Diaries
It Happened Last Wednesday
A Frickin' Fantastic Friday
A Tantalizing Tuesday

Standalone
Santa's Big Helper
A Menu For Loving
North to Alaska
Turning the Page
An Untitled Love
Wyoming Nights
Montana
Blind Date
The Christmas Quilts

Watch for more at ogaines.com.

DAVONSHIRE HOUSE
Publishing Company

Davonshire House Publishing
PO Box 9716
Augusta, GA 30916

© 2014 Olivia Gaines, Cheryl Aaron Corbin
Copy Editor: Teresa Thompson Blackwell
Cover: Corbin Media
Olivia Gaines Make Up and Photograph by Latasla Gardner Photography

ISBN-13: 978-0692325124 (Davonshire House Publishing)
ISBN-10: 0692325123
ASIN: B00O1B1LRA
Printed in the United States of America
1 2 3 4 5 6 7 10 9 8
First Davonshire House Publishing October 2014

DEDICATION
To Terri. Teresa. Theresa...Oh hell; however, you spell it!

Thank you for getting past the initial meeting and coming out on the other side with me. Much love!

ACKNOWLEDGMENTS

For every woman who understands the standard, and will not settle for less. Here is your happily ever after.

A special thank you for putting up with my million questions:

Adventureland Safari Tours – Barbados
The Party Boat- St Lucia
ATV Island Tour and Orient Beach Tour - St. Maarten

Just breathe...

"That's it Sweetheart, you are doing great. Just breathe..." Nigel stood beside the bed holding onto his wife's hand as she tried to breathe her way through the sharp pains. "You are doing fantastic. We are almost there," he told her as he mopped her sweat-soaked brow with a damp cloth.

"Oh God, Oh God, forgive me for my sins," Wilhelmina yelled out as the next sharp pain soared through her lower extremities like a thief in an open jewelry market. "I am going to die. I am not going to make it." She told her husband and she held on to the pillows, her head lolling from side to side.

"Here Love, take my hand, take my hand" he said as her fingers gripped his hand. The next pain that came forced her to clamp down and almost bite the hand that was helping her. The nurse tried not to laugh as Nigel yelled out, "Oh, oh, owww, let go of my hand, let go of my hand!"

The doctor, who had been quiet until this point, said, "Okay Milady, you are starting to crown; it is time."

Wilhelmina was beyond reason, "It's time! What do you mean it's time? It has been time for the past nine hours. Somebody get this child out of me!"

Nigel kissed her forehead, trying to help her remain calm, "Okay Sweetheart, on the count of three, I want you to bear down and push with everything you have," he told her as he gripped her hand again, mumbled words of encouragement and counted down. "One, two, three, push!" Wilhelmina gave it everything she had and pushed. "Great, Sweetheart, the head is out. Now we have to get his shoulders out as well. Again, by the numbers, we go again."

"I'm so tired Nigel. Can't you just reach in there and pull him out? Tell him his Mommy needs a nap..."

The love that he felt for his wife radiated through his pores. "We want to make sure he is not hurt during the process Sweetheart. You can do it, you are one of the strongest women I know. Okay, on my count."

She pushed hard and within seconds she heard his first cry. Their son was born. Vanity Devons was now a mother.

{1} London Calling...

"**G**ood Morning," the sultry British voice on the other end of the line said. "Last night I was hit with an absolutely brilliant idea," he said with entirely too much cheer in his voice.

Vanity Devons sat behind her desk twisting a piece of silk cording, "And what would that idea be Your Grace?" Nigel Strathmore, the fifth Duke of Glastonbury and the owner of Strathmore Textiles took pleasure in his bi-weekly calls to her. She took more of a liking in taunting him with formalities.

"I have decided that I am going to marry you," he said with confidence as if he had just discovered a revolutionary new stain-resistant fabric.

"And I am going to agree with this brilliant idea yours?" she asked with some facetiousness.

"Yes, because I am going to sweep you off your feet in a grand romantic gesture and remind you for the rest of our lives, why you fell head over heels in love with me," he told her. Vanity could also hear his smile through the phone.

"I think I missed out on something, Your Grace. And when did I fall in love with you?" She did actually like the man more than most she met. He was one of the few men who did not objectify her or treat her like a pretty face attached to a pair of boobs and a working receptacle for their prodding intentions.

As the owner of a lingerie company and former model, it no longer shocked her when men assumed she was stupid or a sex toy — or a combination of both—a stupid sex toy. There were several men who were blatant if not disrespectful in their approach to her, but David, her big brother, had taught her that those types of men are waiting for a response. He told her, "It diminishes the punch if the receiver is unfazed by the blow." It took her a couple of years, but she learned how to shield her face and not give anything away in her expressions, unless she was on camera.

Nigel Strathmore was like a great photographer. Within 15 minutes of meeting her, he had disarmed and lowered her defenses. An hour later they were deep in conversation and by the end of the evening she had let her hair down, figuratively, and he was running his fingers through her trademark tresses. It was very unlike her to allow a man such liberty, but for some odd reason, she felt safe with him.

"You started falling in love with me the first time I held you and gazed deeply into those hazel eyes while I ran my fingers through that glorious hair of yours," Nigel lowered his voice a few octaves as he allowed the words to roll across his sexy lips.

"So, is that all you have Sir Nigel?"

"What do you mean is that all I have? I am proposing to you, declaring my intentions for your heart. Wilhelmina, I am crushed," there was a chuckle in his voice. Each time he called, they would discuss business, but his last few calls had been more of a personal nature, but Vanity knew it was a dangerous game of cat and mouse. Nigel Strathmore was a man who was after more than her pretty face and body. He wanted something more from her that he seemed intent upon having. He captured her attention by being one of the few people to call her by her given name of Wilhelmina versus her public persona, Vanity Devons.

She tried to hide her facial expressions so her staff wouldn't see her reaction to the call, "Well, last week the Sultan of Brunei offered to make me his third wife and build me a glass high-rise of monumental proportions in the desert as a token of his love for me." She pressed her lips tightly together to keep from laughing as she said the very true words.

"Third wife, eh? Somehow I don't see you being comfortable as anyone's third choice," Nigel told her.

"That is true. Well, the week before that, Australian business magnate Rocko Deblasse sent me a plane ticket, an eight-carat emerald engagement ring and a 20 pound chocolate candy heart." It was hard not to grin as she said the words because Nigel was definitely going to break his regal composure on that one. And he did.

"DeBlasse? The earthworm farmer?"

"Yes, that would be him..."

"Darling, the man made a fortune shoveling shit-eating earthworms. Which is what you will probably need after eating 20 pounds of chocolate!"

Vanity could not contain her laughter. Nigel lowered his voice again, becoming sultry once more as he planted a mustard seed, "I could listen to the sound of your laughter all day and all night."

The line was quiet. "Wilhelmina," he whispered into the phone.

"Yes, Your Grace?"

"I plan to marry you twice. First in your country and then in mine," he said it in such a way that her heartbeat skipped its normal rhythm.

"That is going to be hard to do, isn't it, considering you don't like to fly, especially for such a long trip over the pond? Then you would have to fly half way across the continent, since I am headed to Arizona, then on to Nevada," she whispered back to him.

"For the woman who will be the mother of my children, the caretaker of my heart, and my lifelong companion... I would cross the desert on a giant shit-eating earthworm for your love," he told her as her laughter cascaded through the phone.

"Wow, Your Grace, I don't know what to say," she spoke through her laughs.

"You can start by saying my name, Wilhelmina."

The line was quiet again.

Vanity exhaled softly, preparing her face as if she were selling a bottle of romantic lotion for two. She braced herself and got into character as if she were about to deliver the quintessential line in a movie scene. She allowed her throat to become breathy as she spoke his name, "Nigel..."

She heard his voice catch through the phone. "I'm coming for you my love. I will see you soon."

And with that he hung up.

Hmm... He called me Darling.

Nigel Strathmore was getting personal.

{2} Feel this...

Vanity sat behind the desk in her New York office, pondering Nigel's words. As much as she wanted to discard the proposal, she could not. Something about his request felt as genuine as the man himself. Me... married to Nigel Strathmore. That was about as funny as being the third wife of the Sultan or being married to a man who played with earthworms all day.

It was nothing new to her to receive marriage proposals. They came often since she was 12 years old. One man in South Africa offered to buy her from her brother for half a million. Another in Malaysia with less means offered her brother David a goat, two ducks, and bag of corn kernels. To her it wasn't flattering. Much of it she found offensive, being diminished to a collectible love toy, which, looking as she did, was expected. Whether she wanted it or not.

David, who had also served as her manager and later business partner, was shocked when she confided her dream to start a high-end lingerie company. "I am going to be objectified either way. This way I can control the images and make a decent living," she told him.

The living she made was more than decent. Her company, Vanity's Pleasure, and products were the haute couture of underwear, designing exclusive lines of lingerie for extremely wealthy clients. She used only the finest silks, satins, and high-end fabrics, which Strathmore Textiles made. The meeting between Nigel and her was arranged by David as a first step in exploring a potential business relationship with his new line of silks. The initial meeting in London had been arranged and Vanity traveled to the factory with her twin brother Wilfred.

Initially, Vanity saw nothing different about Nigel. She seldom gazed upon men for their looks, which was the last thing to catch her eye. Her brothers were two of the most handsome men she knew and no man was more handsome in her mind than her father, so all others paled in comparison. However, Nigel, she began to notice his features right away. He was a fine-looking man. Tall, with dark hair and blue eyes. He had a full bottom lip and an intense stare that called to the woman in her. It didn't seem to not matter what his question was, she always had a ready answer to anything he wanted to know.

On the first night of the day they met, during a quiet evening in front of a soft fire in Strathmore Keep, the family home, she caught a glance of the real Nigel. Rarely, if ever, she was left alone with a man. Not only by her request, but also by her brother's design. Yet, on this night, she wanted a moment alone with the famed haberdasher. She was glad she did.

He let down his guard and she, her hair, which drew him to her like a moth to a campfire lantern. Never had she allowed a man to run his hands through her trademark hair, but in his hands she was relaxed, which was something she seldom was in the company of men. In some ways she expected him to turn on her and attack, but he was a complete gentleman, as she would expect from a man who grew up in a castle.

Strathmore Keep was a bit of a family museum more than a home. It housed vaults, wine cellars, secret passages, and art that had not been seen in centuries. "Is that Anne Boleyn in the painting," she asked him, pointing at the framed art above the fireplace.

"Yes, it is," he said with a stern look on his face. "Although I do say, even for a cousin, she is a very unattractive woman."

Vanity moved closer to the painting, "But the jewelry she is wearing is amazing, especially that ring."

Nigel moved in and stood closer to Vanity, looking at the woman next to him instead of the painting, "I say it is rather unique and extremely beautiful..."

"I have never seen anything like it," she continued to stare at the painting, knowing he was looking at her.

He exhaled softly, his breath caressing the side of her face, "it is indeed a rare treasure." Vanity turned and their eyes met. He only held the gaze for a moment before giving her a slight bow and bidding her good night.

The next day as they left his castle and flew to Milan, her plane had a slight malfunction and required a part for the landing gear.

Nigel was very gracious, "Ms. Devons, you, your brother, and pilot are welcomed to stay at my villa while you await your repairs. I will get my mechanic to personally handle it and get you safely across the pond," Nigel said with confidence. It took three days to repair the plane. Both her pilot, Chuck and her brother knew the repair could have been completed in a day, but Nigel wanted more time with her.

It was not a red flag for Vanity. She also wanted more time with him.

NIGEL SAT BEHIND THE antique desk in the factory his great-great-great grandfather had built in the early 1800's. The old building had been retrofitted, updated, and maintained presently employing nearly 150 people. The fabrics produced at this facility were used to make mattresses, ticking, and draperies. The Milan factory produced higher end silks and materials for clothing manufacturers. The leathers used by notable shoe makers were treated and prepared in the Verona factory. All in all, Nigel had maintained a business he inherited and loved. The issue was to find a woman who loved him and understood what he did. There were many women who wanted to get in on his game, but he wasn't willing to play with his life's work.

An afternoon in the company of Vanity Devons was a game changer for him. She knew fabrics and spoke his business language. On a more personal note, she understood his dry humor and was a well read and learned woman. It also helped greatly that she was absolutely the most beautiful creature he had ever met in his life. The photos of her did not do her any justice since they failed to capture the light that emitted from her spirit. What he loved most was that she was seldom in makeup. Her natural skin glowed healthily and she had a quick wit and ability to speak intelligently on subjects from high finance to human trafficking. She was indeed a special woman.

"I truly enjoy talking to you," he remarked over a small breakfast of coffee and poached eggs.

"And I, you," she replied, pushing the eggs about her plate.

She said nothing more and Nigel knew at that moment she was the woman for him. There wasn't a string of questions after each sentence he spoke, just a simple reply, which is why he liked talking to her. Refreshing.

"I noticed you are not a big eater," he said as he forked in a bite of the Eggs Benedict.

Her eyes came up to meet his, "I eat my fair share. I just don't really care for eggs."

Nigel's curiosity was peaked, and he thought he would gauge her sense of humor. "I have often wondered myself who the first person was to think it was a good idea to eat the white thing that dropped out of a chicken's arse."

Vanity's eyes sparkled as she laughed at his statement. "Or, who was the genius who thought to use the contents of that little white container as a binding agent when added to flour, sugar, salt, and butter to make a sweet and tasty treat?"

Her laughter was like magic dust to his sagging heart. It began to beat at a rapid pace. That laughter... he wanted more of it. He chose each word carefully as they spoke. Even during a bit of a heated debate over the benefits of Egyptian cotton over Pima blends, he was completely stimulated by their banter. But it wasn't easy figuring out how to unlock the chamber that housed the essence of Vanity Devons.

It took at least a day to understand how to communicate with her since she gave away very little with her facial expressions, but those eyes, those hazel eyes were like pools of liquid silver that called to him. And that hair. She has been taught well how to comport herself around men.

Initially, Nigel thought it was an automated response to her looks that drew him in, but her brain kept his attention. Even when they were in his home during her first visit, they argued about fabric. Not wanting to back down, yet thoroughly enjoying the exchange, he went to his home office and pulled out a sample of the Egyptian and Pima Cotton blends, sticking both in her face, daring her, "Feel this... and tell me if your argument stands."

Her hair was unbraided and hanging loose down her back. She grabbed a hunk of it and stuck it in his hand, "The difference in the two are as different as the feel of my hair in your hands and that of a horse's mane."

She was right. "Can you feel the difference?" She asked, staring him in the face. There were many feelings coursing through him as he held the strands of hair in his hand with her standing so close. "I can feel what you are saying..." He wanted to sense so many more things with her.

The kissed she planted on him before she left Milan maintained his interest to the point of distraction. Yet, what he wanted from her was something more permanent. Vanity Devons made him want something he was never before interested in having. A family.

I want to make her my wife.

{3} Ready or Not...

The desk was covered in fabric swatches, bolts of silk, and rough sketches, and the tension in Vanity's shoulders was making her muscles stiff. The Milan show was right around the corner and the changes would keep her up at night sewing, adjusting, and making last minute corrections. If push came to model shoving, she would model the designs herself. Her small team was at her side, minimizing distractions as she measured, measured again, and cut once. She heard the phone lines ringing, but refused to even look up from what she was doing. If it was something important, she would be notified. Right now, what was important was this show and the new line of silks from Strathmore Textiles. She had overspent on the materials, but it was necessary to make sure no one else had the fabric patterns she had purchased. Exclusivity was her trademark, and her meals depended on staying true to her brand.

"Vanity, I have Nigel Strathmore on line 2 for you," her assistant Jessica said through the speaker phone. She could almost feel the tension leaving her body and her shoulders coming down when she hit the button and heard his wonderful British accent.

"Good Morning, Nigel," she said softly, the speaker still on as she maneuvered her way around her office.

"Did I catch you at an inconvenient time? You sound almost distressed."

Vanity put the scissors down on the table and walked around her desk, "I'm okay. I just have a lot to do before my brother's wedding next week. Then I'm due in Vegas right after that..." she sighed into the air, hoping saying the words out loud would alleviate some of her stress. "Enough about me, how are you doing today?"

"I was thinking about getting away from all of this for a mini holiday, you know, changing the pace for a bit."

Vanity listened closely to what he was not saying, "What is a bit for you Nigel?"

Her voice, so melodious to his ears made him open the calendar app on his computer to check his schedule. "If I rearrange a couple of things, I could get away for about 5 days or so."

That made her laugh. "And what are you planning to do for about 5 days or so, Your Grace?"

The line was quiet.

Vanity was learning that his quietness meant he was thinking. His thinking meant he was planning.

"Vegas," he said. "That is the place where Americans are always jetting off to and getting married?" He asked her to wait for a minute as he spoke with someone in the background.

"Wilhelmina, my apologies, I am back," and she could hear him clicking away at his keyboard.

He was up to something and she was intrigued, "Nigel what are you doing?"

"Changing my schedule, which means now," he paused and she heard the clicking of keys again. "I will have about 10 days or so."

"You still haven't told me what you are planning on doing with the time you are allocating." As she said the words, she looked in the mirror across the room and noticed the scowl on her face. I don't scowl.

"I'm planning to start a life with you," he said calmly.

"Is that so?"

"Yes, it is so."

The laughter wafted through the room so loud and bright that both her assistant and Clarke, her makeup and set designer, turned to look at her. Nigel took the reins of the pony, gently kicked the flanks and rode it on home. "I thought we covered this already, Wilhelmina. I plan, with grand romantic gesture, to sweep you off your feet, ask your father for your hand in marriage, and whisk you off to Vegas to make you my wife."

"I thought we covered this already as well, Nigel. What makes you think I am going to agree to your proposal?"

"Because you're falling in love with me and I cannot seem to make it through the day without needing to hear your voice," he told her in a matter of fact tone.

"Does that mean you are falling in love with me as well, Your Grace?"

Someone in his background was urging Nigel off the phone to get to a meeting. "I must run, Wilhelmina."

"You did not answer my question Your Grace." She toyed with a pencil on her desk and began to doodle on the sheet of paper in front of her.

"I have answered your question, my Darling. I fell hard, deeply and madly the second day I spent in your company, but I must run now," he said.

"Nigel wait..."

"Yes, my Love?"

There was the silence.

"I never said yes to your marriage proposal Nigel," Vanity was trying to sound firm.

"That is because I have not asked in person."

Vanity understood that Nigel flying over the Atlantic was not going to happen. Whatever caused his fear of flying, he wasn't going to overcome it in the next four days. She allowed herself a liberty with him she had not before. "If you truly love me that much Nigel, then come and get me. I will be yours..."

The grinned that formed on his face was almost audible through the line between two continents, "I will hold you to those words Wilhelmina, and I will see you next week at Lake Havasu. Have a wonderful week."

He was gone. Vanity's eyes were wide as shocked registered on her face. Jessica ran into the office, "Vanity, is everything alright? Did you get some bad news?"

She looked at her assistant in disbelief. "Did you happen to mention to the Duke my schedule or where I would be next week?"

Jessica shook her head no. Vanity flipped through the mental transcript of their conversation and she could not remember mentioning exactly where her brother's wedding was taking place. How did he know?

Oh Dear God! What if he actually showed up?

Clarke walked in with a one-legged mannequin with a defective butt cheek. "Who does this remind you of?" he asked.

"Out Clarke!" she chuckled at the reference to a semi-famous British lady who married well.

Vanity dismissed the conversation with Nigel and set to work on the Milan show.

{4} Always a bridesmaid...

The wedding was beautiful, simple, and tastefully done. Vanity had never seen her twin brother Will, look happier and Elsie was absolutely glowing. As a tribute to her twin, she played the wedding march and even sang the wedding song of choice by Elsie, whose taste in music was equal to her taste in clothing. A mental countdown had begun in Vanity's head for her escape from all the overflowing displays of love and happiness, as well as the removal and burning of the hideous yards of periwinkle taffeta fabric that Elsie called a bridesmaid dress. Although she was not one to drink, a shot of vodka, chased by a shooter of Irish Whiskey, and washed down with a swig of cold beer sounded pleasantly refreshing in comparison to the nightmare of pitiful looks which were about to be hurled in her general direction.

It would be only a mere matter of moments before her aunts started in on her about working so hard, being single, and money not being a companion. So beautiful and yet always alone. The evening would only get worse after she danced with her father and was forced to do an Argentine Tango with David. She had already been relegated to sit at the singles' table with Will's haphephobic assistant and Rod's assistant that looked like an unemployed Muppet. I have nothing in common with these women. Fifteen more minutes and she could slide out the side door and slip away to her room.

From the corner of the table, she watched her cousin Khalea dance with her husband Stefano. Although she was only two years older, Khalea was an accomplished attorney, owned her own firm, and was a wife and a mother of two mini hell-hounds, one of whom was chasing a little girl with a rubber snake. At the last family gathering the rubber snake had been replaced with his own little wiener that he held in his hand as he chased several of his girl cousins about the room. The older of the two had a thing for matches and had to consistently be watched closely. Kids. Yeesh! But she did want her own. Lately, the desire to be a mom was rubbing at the back of her hormonal clock like raccoons scratching in a trash bin.

Five minutes more and she was out of here. She made her way to the bar to select her companion for the evening. She was gravitating between Mr. Chardonnay or a French lover, Mr. Chenin Blanc, as companions in her lonely room. The wine was almost in her hands when she heard the sound of the death of her night, "Willie, it's time for Elsie to throw the bouquet! They need all you single girls to line up!"

Oh silk sheets! Just stick a hot poker in my eye. I think it would be less painful.

The bartender could not hide his look of amusement as she hesitantly handed him back the bottle of wine and turned to face her tormentors. A well-rehearsed plastic smile was stuck upon her face as she muddled her way to the mottled crowd of single women. Aunt Sadie had embarrassed her a few months ago at David's wedding by doing the same thing and calling her out as a single lady. The only difference was that David's wife Halley had male coworkers and smooth-talking Southern cousins. Boy did she have a lot of cousins, friends, colleagues, classmates, and fast-talking Jersey Boys. Halley's friends and co-workers were a very diverse crowd with lots of interesting people to chat with during the evening. That wedding was fun, this one, not so much.

Elsie had a small family and her wedding party was limited to two other librarians and a cousin who served as janitor at a middle school in Kennesaw. Normally, it would not matter to her a person's profession, but the man insisted upon sharing the best waxes for high volume floors. "I'll keep that in mind," she told him as she excused herself.

Aunt Sadie pushed Vanity into the forefront of the pack as Elsie turned her back, readying herself to throw the handful of wildflowers. Vanity looked to her left to see more of the periwinkle fabric hanging loosely from the shoulders of the skinniest woman she had ever seen in her life. That said a lot considering she had spent the last seventeen years around models. On the other side was Will's assistant who stood next to the Muppet queen, along with Vanity's cousin Jaelon, the other librarian with the hairy legs, and two other wedding guests.

I am hating life.

Elsie counted to three. The bouquet was up, it was in the air, and it was flying and coming at her face. Vanity raised her hands and instead of swatting it away, she caught it. The bouquet was another reminder of a lonesome night and yet another family function where she was alone with no one to talk to... she let go of the flowers and they hit the floor with a thud. The room was silent and she felt her heart drop along with her spirits.

"I think you dropped something," she heard the British accent and was almost afraid to turn around. The small crowd of women parted and she turned to see the sparkling blue eyes, the regal chin, the thick wavy black hair, and the most perfect set of lips. There were no words needed to express how happy she was to see him, and they stood toe to toe in the middle of the floor. He had come. He had come for her and she made up her mind. I am okay to be his.

She gave him the biggest smile, partly in relief from this nightmare and also because she was genuinely happy to see him. Nigel Strathmore didn't disappoint. In a sharply tailored gray suit, he was a striking figure at six two and even in her high heels, his height was perfect. His thumb caressed her chin as he watched her mouth. "Sorry I am late, but intercontinental traffic was bloody awful."

She wrapped her arms around his neck, leaned fully into him, and initiated the long awaited second kiss. He felt like Heaven against her body and the kiss, oh the kiss swept Vanity Devons off her feet in grand fashion as Nigel dipped her low but held her close. It was a kiss that silenced everyone in the room except her very angry father who walked in and dropped his champagne glass.

David Sr. yelled at the top of his voice, "Who is that man with his mouth on my baby?"

{5} Keeping his word...

T he background music started with a Lionel Ritchie love song, and at the moment, Vanity honestly hated her sister-in-law and her sappy music choices. Nigel extended his hand while asking with his eyes for more than a simple, "Dance with me Wilhelmina." She took his hand and he led her to the dance floor with every eye in the room watching. Vanity felt guilty because this was her twin's night and Nigel was making it theirs. "Nigel, this is Will's night and I will not steal Elsie's limelight."

Nigel felt her pulling back and would not allow her to get away, not this night, not ever. "I just flew nearly 6,000 miles to get to you; allow me the three and a half minutes to come to grips with what I have just done. When reality kicks in, I am going to be buggered," he told her as he held her close and expertly maneuvered her about the floor. The trademark scent she normally wore was not present. Instead, something softer and lighter was on her skin. He held the warmth of her hand in his, hoping to slow his racing heart. The warmness of her breath against his neck whilst holding the woman who was forcing him to conquer his fear of flying, as well as a few others he rarely discussed, drifted him off to a place of serenity.

He battled his claustrophobia in that sardine can of a death to fly across an ocean, then half a continent. Finley, his pilot, landed at LaGuardia to refuel, only to take off again to land in the middle of the desert at some American playground he had never heard of. It was so hot it felt as if he landed on the boilerplate of the heater to Hell. When the jet lag kicked in, he was going to be wiped out, but now he was working on pure adrenaline, his desire to hold her again, and the blossoming love affair he was about to commence. Wilhelmina Devonshire's hand was in his and soon she would be in his life forever. He would hold her tight. He was never going to let her walk away from him again. Nigel moved to the music with her body close enough to feel the heat of her life force, but not close enough to offend or be inappropriate.

She was staring at him, "So you have this all worked out in your head, don't you?"

He smiled at her with a wink, "Yes, my Love, I do. I think you are going to like it as well."

Nigel began by explaining the plan was to first be formally introduced tonight to her family. "However, my Darling, in order for them to be convinced, you are going to have to claim me as the man of your dreams and your one true love," Nigel glanced about the room and spotted her brother David. He nodded his head at him. David gave him a smile.

"Your father is going to question our relationship," he dipped her with a cheeky grin. "You are going to confess to him, 'Oh, Daddy, I love him so... Nigel is the only man for me." He added the last part in a high-pitched girly tone that made her throw her head back and burst out laughing followed by a loud snort. Every head in the room turned once they realized the seldom heard the sound of laughter was emitting from her. As he unrighted her into his arms once more, he spotted Will and gave him a nod. Will was impressed. He gave Nigel a smile.

He continued his fable by adding, "Then I will ask for your hand in marriage and your father will punch me in the face when I explain that I am marrying you twice." Her brows went up as he twirled her about the floor and pulled her in close once more. "When I tell him that we are getting married on Monday in Vegas that is most likely the moment he is going to sock me." Nigel looked at David Sr. He gave the man a cursory nod, but only received a frown, a growl, and what looked like mouthed words of "Get your hands off my Baby."

Vanity gasped, but Nigel continued, "Therefore, I will never have the opportunity tonight to explain that he will be able to give you away at our formal wedding in April in England."

Smiling at her, he added, "When I present you with your engagement gift, you are going to look at your father and say Daddy, this is my man, and I'm going to marry him!" He used the high-pitched voice again, which caused an emission of another burst of laughter followed by another snort as he batted his eyelashes at her saying, "Oh Nigel, this is how love feels!"

Her laughter rang out through the large family room. When she was able to finally contain herself, she told him "You are too funny!"

Nigel kissed her on the nose and continued to lead her into the second song after she explained, "My father is not a violent man and I am not a swooning, mushy, featherheaded type of woman."

"That may be the case, but his mind will assume there is a reason for the rush."

Vanity stopped moving, "I am wondering that myself, Nigel."

"The rush is that you and I are perfect for each other, but our challenge will be figuring out how to live together and begin a family."

Vanity's body was heating up and she realized that she was under his spell and needed to get away. Each time she tried to pull away, he dipped, spun, or pulled her in a bit closer. She could feel the power of his thighs touching hers and suddenly she started to feel sweaty. The periwinkle taffeta wasn't helping in the least. The amount of sweat she was starting to produce became noticeable to even him. "Are you okay, my Darling, or is this hideous pound of periwinkle fabric disguised as a frock causing you discomfort?"

She lied and told him it was the dress.

Nigel told her he was in the US for 10 days so they could start their life together. The weekend he planned to win over her parents, and on Monday, he planned for them to do the tourist thing in Vegas after he made her his wife. Then Tuesday, after her special event, they would board his plane and head back to New York. "Those final days in New York, I will get a better understanding of your world and how I can fit into it."

Her eyes went to his, and the tenderness she saw there made her weak, but she had to be strong. "How will I fit into your world Nigel? Have you also planned for that?"

He smiled at her, "The following week you are due in London, where you will meet my staff and my family and see how I live."

Her eyes searched his, "You are planning to make room for me in your life and in your world?"

The music had stopped and everyone was staring at them, "No, I am planning to make you the life of every room in my world."

Her face felt warm, "What makes you think this is going to work, Nigel?"

The music had started again and it was an Argentine Tango. Nigel opened his arms and said, "Let me show you how natural we are together and how beautiful our world can be."

She reluctantly moved forward as he sandwiched her for the first moves around the floor. Nigel was a surprisingly good dancer as he took her through a Molinete, a sweep, and a single axis turn. Vanity moved with ease and grace with him without any words. He maneuvered her through several colgadas and slowly moved her into a grapevine. Instinct had her raise her leg, but he caught her thigh, shook his head no, and lowered her leg back to the floor and slid into a back ocho. The family had begun to clap at the beauty of their movements. His hands were on her hips as he took a step back, made a side sweep, and she raised her knees, balancing her weight on his hip, and it appeared as if she was running through the air. The family applauded loudly. He slowed his movements, coming to a standstill as she slid down the front of his body, resting her face upon his abdomen while her legs slid into a midway split. His hands went under her arms, raising her torso upwards until their eyes met. He pulled her inappropriately close and she had never felt so alive. She didn't notice that the music had ended until he stepped back and lowered his head to kiss her left hand.

Nigel stood a foot away from her. "I traveled the distance to come for you. I brought the perfect engagement gift. I asked over the phone, and I will ask you again in the presence of your family to be my wife. I have kept my word. Will you keep yours?"

She found herself nodding yes, simply because he was right. Vanity Devons deserved some happiness. She wanted some babies. She wanted a husband. She wanted Nigel and he was here. Good, bad, or ugly, she was going to go with it and they would figure out the rest.

"Great!" He handed her his handkerchief from his breast pocket. "Now be a dear and fetch some ice and put it in here for me." She looked confused but he pushed her towards the bar. "Don't dawdle Darling. We need the ice right away."

Vanity didn't question him as she headed for the bar to fill the handkerchief with ice. She was uncertain if her father was capable of violence, but she was going to be prepared. She tried to work quickly as the cousins closed in and began to pelt her with questions.

"Who is he?"

"How long have you been dating him?"

"Did you two take dance classes?"

The questions stopped once she heard her mother's scream, looked about, and saw Nigel on the floor, flat on his back in front of her father, his nose spouting blood.

VANITY KICKED OFF HER heels and took off running with the hanky full of ice. She reached Nigel's side and was happy for the excess fabric from the periwinkle nightmare she wore. She used the tail of it to wipe away the blood from his perfect Patrician nose. A small Asian woman materialized out of nowhere, unwrapping two tampons that she used to shove up the Duke's nose to stave off the bleeding. The strings were dangling freely about his lips, looking like two strands of uncaught snot.

Her father was furious, yelling at her brothers, yelling at Chuck, yelling at her mother. He asked each of them, "How did this happen?"

Everyone was talking at the same time trying to provide the patriarch an answer to what he thought might have happened and how it may have occurred, but honestly, no one was sure what was happening.

David attempted to explain that Nigel was the fourth Duke of Strathmore and the current Duke of Glastonbury.

David Senior was not phased. "I don't care if he is the Duke of Earl. How long has this been going on with your sister?"

Vanity had had enough of her father overreacting, "Daddy stop this right now!" She applied the ice to Nigel's nose as he nestled his head in her lap.

"Nigel is my..." she looked down at him and he stared back waiting for her words, "he's my fiancé."

Nigel looked rather foolish with the two wads of feminine care shoved up his nose as he winked at her, the strings falling into his mouth. There were oohs and ahhs from the crowd.

Will seemed suspicious and was the first to ask, "Well, where's the ring?'

Vanity looked down at Nigel, who was attempting to regain some of his dignity. It was difficult to look distinguished with the whole tampon thing going on, everyone yelling and talking at the same time and Vanity's bridesmaid dress covered in his blood. Nigel scrambled to his feet, and held the ice to his nose, then he took a knee and removed a small black box from his pocket. Before popping the question, Nigel looked at David Senior, "Sir, if I may have your blessing?"

"You don't need to ask my blessing, it's up to her!" David Senior was still fuming and not giving an ounce. Nigel forged ahead.

He opened the box and Vanity's eyes widened at the contents inside, "Is that...."

Nigel nodded, looking even more ridiculous as he blew out a puff of air to move the tampon strings away from his mouth.

"It's just like the one in the painting," she said as he removed the ring from the box to slip on her hand.

It gave him pleasure to tell her, "It is the one in the painting."

Vanity's eyes fill up with tears as she admired the ring he held in between his fingers. Nigel, still on bended knee, asked, "Wilhelmina, will you be my wife?"

Tearfully, she said, "Yes, yes I will," as he slipped the ring on her left hand. She threw herself into his arms, knocking the ice pack from his hand and showering his bloodied face with kisses. "Oh Nigel, yes, yes I will." Vanity looked up at her father. "Daddy, this is my man, and I'm going to marry him!" The new couple both looked at each other and burst into laughter.

As Elena Devonshire wiped away a tear, and David helped his soon to be brother-in-law up from the floor. Will only looked at him and said, "Well, Nigel, when I invited you to my wedding, I really didn't expect you to come."

David's eyebrows went up. "I invited him as well, and I didn't think he would come either."

Vanity was surrounded by cousins who were admiring the ring which had belonged to Ann Boleyn. She tried to answer the plethora of questions being hurled at her about her fiancé but she was so happy, she was stuttering over her words. Nigel's eyes barely left her face as he answered both of her brothers, "It was her invitation that I could not refuse."

Nigel offered his hand to David Senior, who reluctantly accepted it with a glower. Elena Devonshire watched with amusement as the young man she would soon call son, took her daughter into his arms and wielded her around the dance floor. It took a special kind of man to do what Nigel Strathmore had done, and doing it with two tampons sticking from his nose made him a special breed. He was the right man for her daughter without a doubt and soon the world would also find out as well.

Vanity Devons was officially engaged.

{6} Beginning the Journey...

Vanity awoke feeling tired, excited, and anxious all at one time. Last night had been full of surprises, and for a moment she felt as if she had been dreaming. Her hand slowly crept out from under the covers as she incrementally turned her head to glance at her left hand. As her eyes traveled the room, she took another look at the blood-soaked periwinkle fashion faux pas resting on the chair and confirming it was all real. *Nigel is in America and I am engaged.* The beautiful ring on her left hand also confirmed she was getting married.

Vanity turned over into a lump that reminded her that she was sharing the bed with her cousin Jaelon. Since Will left last night to begin his honeymoon, Nigel had taken his room, and Finley his pilot had taken Jaelon's, which meant she and Vanity had to double up. Nigel was very surprised when she offered for Finley to stay at the family vacation home with him. "Do you trust him with your life?" she asked Nigel, who quickly answered yes.

"Well, that makes him family. I am a firm believer in family and family sticks together." Vanity really didn't give him an opportunity to reply, but set about getting them both settled for the evening before giving her new fiancé a promising kiss goodnight. That was last night in the midst of a flurry of excitement.

This was a new morning and a new day. She quickly showered, and then gathered her things and headed down to breakfast. She was surprised to find that Nigel was already awake and standing on the veranda having a cup of tea with David.

"There are smoothies already made if you want one," David told her as she walked forward to greet them both. She stood between the two men in her life uncertain of what she should do, and they both leaned in to kiss her on either cheek.

David informed her, "Finley has gotten together with Chuck and they are both headed to Phoenix to refuel, and later Chuck will bring him over to the house." Vanity nodded and excused herself to head to the kitchen to fuel up her belly before the trip. Over her shoulder she called to Nigel, "We should be ready to roll out in about 20 minutes." They were going to be driving Will's car to her parent's house for the weekend and store it there until he and Elsie returned from their honeymoon in a week. Initially, Gianni and Jordan were scheduled to drive the car to her parents, but she had decided to drive the car last night after agreeing marry Nigel.

I agreed to marry Nigel! Hot fuzz balls on silk!

The drive to Phoenix would give them ample time to iron out some very critical details.

NIGEL WAS DRESSED IN lightweight wool slacks and a baby blue polo style shirt. He had with him an overnight bag and appeared ready to go. He followed her quietly to the garage where she asked him to wait while she fired up the engine of Will's Cadillac and drove it out to meet her new fiancé. My fiancé.

Nigel stood transfixed by the sleek black car with the shiny silver rims and silver trimming. "What is this modern piece of American beautiful?" he asked.

"It is a 2013 Cadillac CTS," she added as he slid into the leather seat on the passenger side, "Her name is Guinevere."

"She is so lovely and she has a name?"

"Yeah, it's Will's thing. He names all of his vehicles." She said no more and she tooted the horn at David and the rest of the family as they drove down Devonshire Lane and headed towards Highway 95. She had meant to leave earlier to avoid the heat of the day, but her mind was racing. They were finally alone and there was much to say, much to discuss and so many things to work out. She and Nigel would have nearly three hours to talk about a great many things. It was still cool enough to let down the windows and Nigel seemed to relax in the seat.

"Wilhelmina, how long is the drive to your parents' home?" He wanted to know as he looked through compartments for music.

"What are you looking for?" she asked, trying to figure out why he was going through her brother's car.

"Music, to commemorate the beginning of our journey..." as he turned and looked at the backseat.

"What is your preference for our journey, classical, techno, eighties?"

He only smiled as he replied, "I actually prefer smooth jazz."

"Smooth jazz, coming up," she vocalized a few commands and the dashboard lit up: "Sirius, Watercolors, volume 5. And we should arrive to our home in about 3 hours." The music began to play and she opened up the engine to about 70 miles per hour, headed towards the Williams Wildlife Refuge, onto LaPaz and then to I-10 into Phoenix.

Nigel was impressed with how she handled the vehicle and fifteen minutes passed with nothing more than silence between them, but he was not going to open the conversation. He would allow her to decide which issues she wanted to address or tackle first. And there were many. However, his priority for making the relationship work was probably not at the top of her list and vice versa.

She looked at him.

He looked at her.

He stared out the window and waited.

"We need to talk about sex," she blurted out. Her hands gripped the steering wheel tightly as she approached a very uncomfortable subject. In the back of her mind, it was an area that had to be handled up front so there were no misunderstandings. In truth, they didn't really know each other. Yes, the two of them were engaged. Yes, their wedding was on Monday, but she was not ready to jump in bed with him. *That is so weird but it makes so much sense.*

"I have our entire lives to make love to you; there is no rush," he added calmly while he hummed along with a Norman Brown version of a Luther Vandross song.

"Well, I don't like it!" She stated defiantly.

He turned in the seat to give her his full attention. "You don't like what... having to wait?"

Her knuckles were turning white as she gripped the wheel harder, "No, I don't like sex. I am lousy at it." *It was out. I said it out loud. Nigel is going to dump me before we even get down the road.*

Nigel was quiet. She waited for his response. A few minutes passed by and he asked her to explain why.

"Men automatically assume that since I make lingerie, I am some amped up sex toy," her eyes were wide when she glanced over at him, "I'm not promiscuous!"

Vanity continued, "I have only been with one man." This brought a wide smile to Nigel's face. Vanity wanted to know, "What's with that grin?"

"It means I don't have to contend with the ghosts of boyfriends past," he pried her fingers from the steering wheel and slipped her hand into his. There were questions he wanted to ask, but he felt they had time. He wanted to get to know her and wanted her to get to know him. If that meant that sex went to the back burner, so be it. "Wilhelmina, sex is a viable part of a relationship and definitely a part of marriage, but it is not what will define us, or our relationship."

Her hand relaxed a bit. "So, you are not that into sex either?"

Nigel's lips were pursed together, shaking his head no, "I thoroughly enjoy sex. I mean we could pull over right now if you were ready," he licked his bottom lip and gave her a look that made her blush, "but I want a life with you, which means, I wait until you," he paused, giving her hand a squeeze. "or rather, we, are ready."

The words all sounded full of flowers and promise. In the dark with a raging hard on, a man could care less about your feelings. Her two years with Stephen had taught her to put it off as long as she could, then just close her eyes and wait until he was done. The sweat was starting to form on her brow. "Nigel, what if I am truly lousy at pleasing you and you don't like how I am in bed?" Her question was posed in almost a whisper.

He kissed her hand, "Then that would mean that I was lousy at it as well." Nigel smiled at her and only added, "It is my responsibility to make sure we are both equally satisfied. More importantly, to make sure that you find your pleasure." He smiled at her and explained that if it took two weeks or two months, then they would wait, "But we figure it out and decide together. When the time comes, Wilhelmina, I will make it a good experience for you." His glance was short but full of meaning as he turned his head and gazed back out of the window.

Vanity removed her hand from his and said, "Lana Turner, a famous American actress once said that a gentleman is nothing more than a patient wolf."

"Yes, but wolves are animals of opportunity which prey upon the weaknesses of lesser animals. You and I have a voyage together. My plans are to date you for a while before I let you chat me up with your big pretty words and fabric talk and get in my pants." Vanity's outburst of laughter was like pixie dust in the air. It was almost infectious. Nigel held up a well-manicured finger into the air, "Because I'm not promiscuous either!" He found himself laughing along with her as well as noticing she physically relaxed as they headed towards a long stretch of empty desert.

When her laughter ebbed, cautious eyes glanced his way, "So. You are planning to date your wife?"

He put on a Texas accent, "Yessiree Bob! And I'm a'gonna date you for the rest of our lives." And there it was—that look that made her go all soft inside. *I can see myself loving this man with everything I have.*

"Now I have a question for you, my darling Wilhelmina." He saw her physically tense up again. She gave him a half smile, encouraging his inquiry.

"Where in the bloody hell are we? I swear I think we just passed that same exact cactus 45 minutes ago..." He pointed at a tall Saguaro. Her laughter rang out, filling the car with a new energy.

His thumb gently rubbed her hand, "Darling, I have never driven an American car before—can I give Guinevere a go?"

Vanity slowed the car and pulled over to the shoulder, "Just remember which side of the road to drive on, okay?"

As they stepped outside of the car, the mid-morning sun hit Nigel like a blow to the chest. "I know where we are... we are at the precipice of the gateway to Hell," Nigel told her as he closed her car door and sauntered around to the driver's side to slid in the seat. He checked the mirror, making a fish face. "I think the skin on my face just shrank from the heat outside," he told her.

My husband. Nigel Strathmore is going to be my husband.

Vanity Devons was getting married.

{7} Dealing with Daddy...

The GPS guided them onto I-10 and straight into Scottsdale to her parent's gated community. Mr. Billy was excited when he saw the black coupe with the Davonshire House trademark logo on the front license plate. He was even happier when Nigel rolled down the window and he saw Vanity's face. In his jolly Texas drawl he said, "I do declare, Ms. Devonshire, you seem to get prettier each and every time I see you, child!" She thanked him for the compliment and introduced Nigel as her fiancé.

"Lawd, the press must not have gotten hold to that bit of info yet, Ms. D. I know there will be a world full of brokenhearted young fellas knowing that you are no longer on the market." She only smiled again and waved as she and Nigel slowly began to pull away. "You are a lucky guy there, young man."

"Why, that I am Mr. Billy. Yes, I am." Vanity's jaw dropped as Nigel presented a perfect New Yorker accent.

"It is easier sometimes to just blend in," he said while following the directions of the voice on the GPS.

To Nigel, the gated community looked like every picture he had seen of American suburban living. Each home looked pretty much like the next one with graveled front yards adorned by desert plumage until the GPS guided him down a side street into a cul-de-sac. In the half circle lay a home that was definitely outside the norm. It was an unusual shade of green trimmed in orange, with large windows, and it appeared to be a botanical garden of desert foliage and plants. Vanity instructed Nigel, "Pull into the drive and drive around back to the garages."

The press of a button on the steering wheel opened the garage door on the end. Nigel skillfully maneuvered the car into the garage and killed the engine. "Guinevere gets great gas mileage," he said as he removed their bags from the car. "Do I need to have her serviced, washed or have petrol added?"

"It will be taken care of—come let's go inside." As she started to walk away, Nigel noticed there were five cars in the garage. The newest was the one they just parked. There was an SUV, which was probably her father's, a mid-sized sedan, which probably belonged to her mother, Will's caddy, an old Jeep, and a well- maintained Nissan. "Which one is yours?" he asked.

Vanity pointed to the Jeep and smiled. Nigel was surprised. The vehicle was nearly seventeen years old. "It is rather timeworn, isn't it?"

"It runs like a charm," she said, eyeing the car as if it was the newest and most expensive model.

"Do you have another vehicle other than this one?" Nigel eyed the older automobile and could not imagine this beautiful woman driving such an outdated lorry. He would soon buy her another fitting of her beauty and social standing. She was going to be a Duchess.

She touched the car with a fondness that radiated through her smile, "This was my first and only car. My father gave this to me for my 16th birthday." She looked at him with mists of tears in her eyes, "When I am here, I don't drive, and besides, I seldom go anywhere alone."

Nigel realized that her life was far more complicated than he may have initially thought. The next ten days in America in her world would give him a better understanding of the woman he would soon call his wife. She was definitely nothing like he had imagined. She was very modest and not prone to excess. He peered over her shoulder and eyed the house. Her parents were well off. From what he had read, her father was some form of Lord Chief Justice. David was an executive, and she was a multi-millionaire, but the house, was...well normal looking from the outside. Her twin...I don't know what that chap does for a living. The inside would really tell how her parents lived and how she had been raised. His decision to plan this trip to claim her as his bride was feeling better and better. It had been a while since Nigel had been this excited about anything in his life. The next few days were going to be stimulating and he could barely wait.

He followed her towards the back door of the house, unknowing that the next ten minutes would change his life in more ways that he had anticipated. Starting the moment he stepped through her parent's patio door.

THE BACK PORCH HELD a massive gas grill, a roaster, a charcoal grill, and an awning with a hot tub next to very comfortable lounge furniture. The garden was lush and almost out of place. It seemed a bit extravagant for a desert home but then he noticed the filters and realized the garden was being watered with a recycling system. The arbors that covered the plants helped keep them cool and whoever designed the garden had taken a great deal of care in its planning.

Vanity did not interrupt him as he took it all in. She waited patiently by the door until he had completed his inspection of the mini oasis. "David hired his gardener to install all of the plants, but Gianni designed the irrigation and watering system for Mamí."

"Your brother's teenage son designed the irrigation system?" He looked impressed and turned to follow her towards the door but she had not moved. "Before we go in, I need to tell you about my cousin Cookie," she said with a very low voice.

Vanity explained the Cookie was her father's niece and had been living with them for the last thirty years. "She has a form of Down's syndrome and has no filters."

She said the last part with a smile, "Please don't be offended at anything Cookie says. She has a wonderful heart, and is a great...." he stopped her words with a kiss. She swooned into him a bit, falling into the strength of his chest and he released her and opened the kitchen door.

As they entered the kitchen, a middle-aged black woman stood washing fruit at the sink. She turned and looked at Vanity and her eyes and face lit up, "Willie, you're home. I got lots of fruits and veggies from the market, just like you like!"

Vanity reached into her bag and pulled out a brightly colored scarf, "And for you Cookie, I found this perfect scarf. I thought you would love it."

Nigel watched the scene and was truly touched by Wilhelmina's love for her cousin. He admired the way they spoke to each other and communicated with small exchanges of affection. Vanity tied the scarf around the lady's neck and gave her a big warm hug. "Cookie," Vanity added, "this is Nigel. Nigel and I are going to be married."

Cookie's eyebrows went up. Nigel moved forward to enter her space, "Cookie, it a pleasure to meet you."

"You talk funny!" She said with a surprise in her voice.

Nigel touched her arm and lowered his voice, "That's because I am from England, and most people in England sound like I do."

Cookie stepped back, looking at Nigel as if he had done something wrong. He looked at Vanity, wondering if he had as well. Cookie frowned at him, pointing her finger in an accusatory manner, "Uncle David said you were the son of bitch that was trying to steal his baby!"

Vanity gasped as she heard an audible growl from Nigel, "I'm sorry, what?"

"Uncle David said you were a son of a bitch," she went back to washing her fruit, "Would you like an apple, you Son of a Bitch?"

Vanity turned her head in an effort to collect her thoughts about how to handle this. Instead it was Nigel who spoke and addressed her father's intended jab at him, "Cookie, that is your Uncle David's special name for me, but do you know what Willie likes to call me?"

Her eyes were wide as she handed him an apple, "No, what does Willie like to call you, Son of a Bitch?"

His smile was terse, but Nigel was set upon giving it back to his soon to be father-in-law. "Willie likes to call me her Loverman."

He said it with such a huge smile that Cookie started smiling too. "Cookie, I would like for you to call me Willie's Loverman as well. Can you do that?"

Cookie was smiling back at Nigel, who had taken the apple from her hand and taken a big bite. He told her how it was a good choice and praised her for making such a lovely selection at the market. He made a point of touching everything in the sink and telling her how awestruck he was at her fruit-picking talent. She grinned and pretended to be shy as she sliced an apple and added the perfect tablespoon of peanut butter to a small cup and handed it to Vanity. From his back pocket, he removed a handkerchief that was embroidered with NCS, with the C being prominent. It was made of the finest cotton, and he handed it to Cookie, who noticed the enlarged C.

"C is for Cookie!" She hugged Nigel and acted as if he had given her the gift of sight. Vanity was captivated by the interchange between the two but worried at the same time. Nigel had called her father's play, which meant lunch was going to be tense.

She showed Nigel the house and then took him to the guest room to give him a moment to freshen up before they sat down for a jousting match she was uncertain her fiancé was going to win. She said a silent prayer in hopes that her father and soon-to-be husband could find a happy medium. The remainder of Saturday and all day Sunday, they would spend with her parents before taking off on Monday morning to Vegas.

I just have to get through this.

Getting through it was going to be a bit tougher than she had planned. The doorbell rang and her cousin Khalea showed up with her briefcase. *The briefcase means legal documents and my Daddy is going to go all lawyer on Nigel.*

This was not going to be good.

{8} Say What Now...

Khalea re-introduced herself to Nigel and apologized for leaving so early last night. It was almost lunchtime and her Loverman thanked her father once more for his hospitality and complimented Elena on the home. Cookie walked in with lunch service and Elena rose to help serve the food. Vanity poured the tea while Khalea aided with silver wear. Everyone was busy doing something leaving Nigel and her still very angry father at the table alone.

"Is there anything I can help with?" Nigel asked.

All the women said no, as plates were made and placed first in front of her father then in front of him, next the mother, Khalea, and finally Vanity. Cookie seldom ate at the table, but was smiling at Nigel and he smiled back at her. "Would you like some more tea, Willie's Loverman?"

Elena choked and Khalea dropped her head. He responded nicely to her that he was fine. Cookie was grinning from ear to ear as she took out the handkerchief Nigel had given her and wiped at the corners of her mouth with the embroidered C. Cookie went all soft and batted her eyelashes at Nigel when she told him, "I have some more asparagus in the kitchen if you want some more of that too, Willie's Loverman."

Nigel smiled at her, "Everything looks absolutely divine Cookie. I can't wait to sample your delicious cooking."

She bounded off to the kitchen, yelling over her shoulder, "Okay Willie's Loverman!"

Everyone at the table stared down at their plates with the exception of Nigel, who raised his glass and looked down the table at her father. Vanity slowly raised her eyes and noticed the smirk on her father's face. Nigel raised his glass higher in a toast and her father reciprocated, "Well played, Your Grace."

David Sr. blessed the food and they began to eat.

It was here that Nigel could not help but notice the exact portions on Vanity's plate. Surprisingly, she ate all of her food, and her dessert was a small bowl of strawberries, while the rest of the table had sponge cake with berries and fresh cream. Lunch was rather quiet and Vanity was almost okay with it, knowing why Khalea was here.

Lunch was quickly over and Cookie returned, seeking more adoration from Nigel, who slathered it on her with a very large knife, "The salmon was cooked to perfection and lunch was amazing. Thank you, Cookie, it was fantastic." He patted on his belly.

"Thank you, Willie's Loverman!" she added while collecting the dirty dishes. Vanity gave her a hand with clearing the table and Nigel rose and took his plate to the kitchen as well. "Wilhelmina, everything is so tense. What is happening?"

David Sr. came into the kitchen, "It's because I want to speak with you before you two move forward with your plans." Nigel handed his glass to Cookie to be added to the dishwasher and followed the patriarch back to the dining room.

Still in the kitchen, Vanity watched the two walk away and only hoped that Nigel wouldn't get punched in the nose again. She held onto the glass and Cookie nearly had to fight with her cousin to get the woman to relinquish her grasp. "I had a Loverman once too, Willie," she said very quietly.

Vanity turned to the woman who had spent so many years of her life in this kitchen cooking meals for the family. "Really Cookie, what happened to him?"

"Uncle David tried to shoot him," she said and went back to humming and loading the dishwasher.

Vanity stood dumbfounded, "Say what... now?"

With a face full of concern, Cookie turned to look at her cousin, "He didn't shoot him, though. He wanted to, but I told Uncle David that I loved him, and if he hurt my Jimmy it would break my heart."

She never knew this... any of this. Vanity watched Cookie's face, who turned, her eyes softly framed by grayed temples. "I have been locked in this kitchen for a long time because I was scared of Uncle David. I'm not very smart, but I do know some things. I know love."

Vanity had never heard Cookie speak so plainly before. Over the years, it had only been a few words to her as she prepared her food and asked her to bring specific items she would want to wear, but a heart-to-heart—never.

"If you want to be with your Loverman, go in there and stop Uncle David. If not, you are going to be stuck all alone in the kitchen too!"

KHALEA REMOVED PAPERS from her briefcase, "Nigel, what I have here are called Prenups."

"I am familiar," he told them as Khalea handed him the papers.

Vanity slipped into the room and said nothing as her father and personal attorney explained about protecting the interest of Vanity's Pleasure Lingerie Company as well as Vanity's personal interest. "This just says that if you divorce my baby, you get nothing of hers," David Sr. added.

Nigel reached for the pen that Khalea had, took the documents and looked for his name, and signed them without reading through the details. He then handed the pen to Vanity, "Wilhelmina, darling, your turn."

She stepped up and signed the documents as well, and Nigel kept one copy for himself, folding it putting it in his back pocket. "Right then," Nigel said as he turned towards her mother, "Elena, might I trouble you for a cup of tea?"

Her father was not satisfied. This was not how he was supposed to meet his son-in-law. They were supposed to talk and bond and share stories. Nigel Strathmore was cold and there was nothing that radiated from the man that made David Sr. want to trust him with his daughter. Then to sneak off to Vegas to wed her, without him there to give her away. He probably planned to move her completely to England, a country with no sunshine. With a scowl on his face, he asked, "Will my Pumpkin have to sign a prenup when she gets to England as well?"

Elena must have been prepared as she poured Nigel a cup of tea from the side board. Nigel, tea in hand, looked at David Sr. square in the face and said, "No, she will not, Sir."

He sipped the tea and went on to tell his soon to be father-in-law, "I don't need her to sign anything because she and I will spend our lives together. What is mine will be hers."

In Nigel's mind, there were no means to tell his soon-to-be father-in-law that he was a good man or to establish a measure of trust other than by simply being honest. Honesty was what he was going to give him. "I apologize for us having to meet this way. It is well known that I do not like to fly, but very few people know why."

As a teenager, Nigel told him that he and a couple of his friends were re-turning from holiday in a private plane. The plane crashed into a lake and the aircraft quickly filled with water. "I have never felt so terrified in my life and it felt like it took a lifetime to get those doors opened." He continued, "Two oth-ers and I struggled, but we made it to shore. Our pilot did not, nor did my best mate."

He inhaled slowly, "To this day, Sir, I have a horrific fear of flying, small closed-in spaces, and especially flying over water." Everyone, including Cookie, was listening to him. "Wilhelmina said if I truly wanted to start a life with her, I would have to come and get her." He looked at her with a gaze that melted her heart, made Khalea smile, and her mother hug herself. "Wilhelmina, I am a man of few shortfalls, but, I will confess, that it took two days of hypnosis, a fortnight with a talented acupuncturist, and poor Finley to sedate me to get me on that blooming plane." He smiled as he admitted that he awoke after a refueling landing and took another mild sedative before the takeoff to come to Phoenix. "I am still feeling a bit daft, but I am here. I came for your hand and I have no idea of how I am going to make it home."

He set the tea cup down and walked over to Vanity. "I did all of that because Wilhelmina is the one for me, and I will deal with any obstacle, hurdle, or fear to make her my wife." He held her hands and gazed into her eyes, saying the words for her father's ears but speaking them to Vanity's heart.

"When you find the one Sir, there is never a time like the present to begin a future."

David Senior looked at his wife. His mouth was twisted in a sarcastic puck-er. "This is some bullshit if you ask me! He isn't fooling anybody. He sees the pretty face and wants to marry some fantasy. We live in the real world. Their children will grow up in the real world, and I will be damned if anyone is going to mistreat my children! Especially my baby!"

Vanity was surprised and taken aback by her father's strong emotions, as was Nigel, who spoke up, "Sir, my wife and our children will inherit my titles, my lands, and anything else due my station. I am unclear what you mean..."

David Sr. cut him off, "Look at me young man. Look at me!"

His words were as strong and as large as his steps as he crossed the room to stand toe to toe with Nigel, "I am a black man, which means my daughter is a black woman." He looked at Nigel, waiting for it to come to light. But the Duke was still unclear, and David Sr. was a luminary, "I am saying that to say this..." He paused to drive the point home. "What are you going to do if your children come out as black as me?"

It wasn't even in the blink of an eye before Nigel gave him the answer he needed, "I am going to love them. Our children will be conceived in love and raised in it as well. I and my wife are going to raise our children in a house filled with love, nurturing, and support. I don't care if they are pink, dark brown, or café au lait."

He looked at Vanity, "Well, if they come out orange, then it's her fault—with her love of carrots." He saw the quick smile on David Sr.'s face flash and then disappear at his light jest, but Nigel went on, "I will put a shot through anyone who tries to harm either my wife or my children." Nigel's hands were in his pockets as he stood there looking at Vanity's parents. He wanted them to understand the kind of man he was.

Nigel turned to address the parents of his bride-to-be, "I took a brief holiday to come America to spend time in her world and to understand her life so that we could figure out how to make our life together work. I also needed to sit at your table, Sir and Madam, make eye contact, and break bread with you." David Sr. began to relax a bit. Nigel moved closer. "I would never deny you the honor of giving her away to a man you like and respect. I can only hope to earn both from you. Your daughter will be the future Duchess of Glastonbury. There is a formal ceremony that has to happen in England in April." Elena slipped her hand into her husband's, who stood still letting it all soak in.

"So in April, you are going to marry her again, in your country, in front of all those Royals and high class people, and I get to give her away? Walk her down the aisle in England?"

"Yes, Sir. And three days later will be her formal coronation as Duchess, when she will be presented to my great aunt, the Queen," Nigel said as he looked at the shock on Vanity's face.

Vanity, Elena, and Khalea remained silent as they watched David Sr. walk to the cabinet to retrieve a bottle of Scotch. "Nigel, come with me, son." Each lady exhaled, not realizing they had been holding their breath. "I bought this Scotch 30 years ago when the twins were born. I was saving it to share with her husband." He collected two glasses, "One finger or two?" Nigel held up his index finger and watched him pour them both a drink. The two adjourned to her father's study and she could hear her father ask, "So Nigel, do you fish?"

Khalea embraced her aunt and looked at her cousin, "That is some mighty powerful love there cousin."

Elena embraced her daughter, telling her, "In order to love him back Baby, you will have to let go of a lot more. Trust in the process and trust in him."

Nigel had laid it all out there for her family to hear. He had let down his guard and confessed something very few people knew about him in order to earn her father's trust. It was her turn.

Her mother was right. Vanity Devons was going to have to let down her proverbial trademark hair and love him back.

{9] Up, up, and awake...

It was 9:30 and there was no sign of Nigel. Her parents and Cookie had just left for church and she had hoped to join them, but her concern now went to His Lordship. The small amount of time she had spent with him did not reveal him as a late sleeper. A minute of panic rushed through her and she headed down the hall to the guest room. *Maybe he decided I wasn't worth it and left.* She tapped lightly at the door, waited for a response, and slowly turned the handle.

"Nigel, it's me. Are you decent?" She pushed the door and entered the room. The soft light of the lamp illuminated his face. The blinds were still drawn as he lay in bed, staring back at her, awake, sluggish, and looking a bit green.

Slow to raise his head, his stomach rumbled. Fear gripped him as he worried whether he would either vomit or have to make a run for the loo. "I am sorry love. I seem to be a bit buggered today. You may need to ring for a physician." Vanity said nothing as she turned on the overhead light and walked closer to the bed. After almost twenty years in the modeling industry, there weren't many illnesses she couldn't diagnose or treat with items from the kitchen. Her first move was to check Nigel's legs. She pushed back the sheet and pulled a well-toned, and somewhat hairy leg from under the covers. Using her index fingers, she pressed into the flesh of his calves checking for pitting. *He isn't retaining fluids.* This was good. She tucked the leg back under the cover.

Nigel said nothing as she moved towards his torso and rolled back the covers to expose his chest. Vanity was pleased when she saw he slept in underwear. It made her even happier when she saw it was her new men's line. Practiced hands touched his chest, checking for sweaty or clammy skin. She rolled the covers back a bit more until they rested at the top of the waistband of his boxers. *Boxers are good; he preferred freedom of movement.* Nigel remained still as she examined him.

Nervous hands pulled the tank top free of his boxers to expose his belly. Using four fingers, she pressed along his abdomen for hardness to see if maybe there was bloating. Dealing with models who had a number of eating disorders, she had grown accustomed to knowing what to look for with either cases of diarrhea or constipation. She smiled when she saw that he was okay digestively.

She pulled the covers back up and told him, "I need for you to sit up." She fluffed the pillows behind his back. Finally, she wanted to check his temperature. Vanity used the method her mother used to test for fever by pressing her lips to his forehead. He had remained quiet until this point when he said, "Well Doc, if you want a snog all you have to do is ask." His smile was weak and she understood better than anything what he could not actually express. As his soon-to-be wife, she knew it was her duty to take care of this man, who was now her man.

Nigel told her, "I am just a bit knackered I think, but I shall be up and about in a bit."

She allowed her hand to linger on his cheek, but she told him, "Stay here, I'll be right back."

Nigel could hear her in the kitchen, putting together heavens know what and he wasn't sure what she would come back with, but he felt good that she was concerned about him.

Moments later, she returned with a tray that contained a glass of something that resembled anti-freeze, peanut butter toast, and applesauce. She sat the tray across his lap and pulled up a chair next to the bed. "The liquid will balance out your electrolytes, the peanut butter will pack in some quick protein, and the applesauce will balance your digestive track." She put the glass in his hand, commanding him to drink. He didn't argue and did as he was told and sipped the beverage.

As their eyes met and she smiled at him, she wanted to be lighthearted, but she needed to shift his energy as well as his focus. Their life together would include a great deal of traveling, and each time he had to board a plane he could not be faced with this form of emotional crippling. Once they were married, she would teach him yoga or Tai Chi to help him find balance. Today, she was going to introduce him to something simpler.

"Nigel, are you familiar with cognitive restructuring?" she asked as she opened the container of peach mango applesauce and spooned out a helping.

He opened his mouth to accept the offering. "I am familiar with the practice," he told her as he opened his mouth for another bite.

Vanity went on to explain that she was going to teach him the very basics of the technique. "The past 72 hours have been mentally and emotionally taxing for you, but we are going to replace some of your negative thoughts about flight and travel with positive ones." She handed him a piece of the toast covered in the peanut butter. He accepted and ate it. "You equate flying with a past negative experience, so I am going to restructure your thoughts towards something positive that you can look forward to each time you have to step aboard a plane." She scooped out more applesauce. Like a baby bird, he opened his mouth to take another helping.

"Travel will be a critical part of our life together, and tomorrow is the start of a new adventure," she said softly.

"Tomorrow we board a plane to make our lives together official. After a quick flight to Vegas, I become Mrs. Nigel Collingswood Strathmore the third."

He smiled, crunched on the piece of toast, and said, "Actually, I am the fourth."

She continued to tell him that his request, as of tomorrow night, would come true. He would go to bed, and wake up to his wife. She described in detail all of the things there were to do in Vegas and told him they would be like two kids on holiday, spending the entire day and night playing and having fun.

"Nigel, are you aware that there is a mini replica of the Eiffel Tower in Vegas, as well as a gaudy version of the Caesar's Palace, and the New York, New York is a replica of the streets of the Big Apple?"

Nigel stared at the neon concoction in the glass. "Do they have little beggars running around as well?"

Vanity found herself laughing, "Yes, complete with a Capuchin monkey wearing a red hat along with rotating thunderstorms."

Nigel only murmured, "That I would love to see."

"I do have to do some work while I am there," Vanity continued and talked about the special event at Wynn Hotel & Casino for the hair company she co-owned. Afterwards, they would end their Vegas adventure. "We then board the plane to fly to one of the greatest cities in the world, New York."

She described her flat, her workspace, and the many sights of the city. "It will only be a couple of days, but right after, you have to fly home, to prepare your world to include me in it."

She talked about how she hoped his mother would like her, then asked, "I understand you have a sister as well?"

"I also have a jet setting, good-for-nothing brother. Let's not forget him," he said as he spoke of his siblings, and finally he responded as they compared his brother and sister to her twin and cousin Khalea. Before long they were laughing and the Duke was feeling better and talking about what they would do tomorrow in Vegas. She fed him the remainder of the applesauce and got him to eat the toast and drink the remaining electrolyte solution.

As she collected the tray, she pressed her lips to his with a brief kiss. "I am excited to be your wife. I am eager to start our life together." His eyes were much brighter and she could tell he was feeling better about his decision, but she wanted to make sure he understood that she was ready. "I am very happy you came for me."

She walked to the door and looking over her shoulder said, "Join me in the kitchen when you are ready."

Nigel was still smiling when he called her name, "Wilhelmina?"

The conversation was open and so was her heart. She felt playful and was getting more excited about having a day alone with him tomorrow. "Yes, Your Grace?"

He pushed the covers to the side and slid out of the bed. His thighs were powerful and muscled, as well as his arms, and he looked tussled and sexy as hell. Nigel Strathmore was all hers and tomorrow, she would be his wife. He crossed the small space to stand in front of her. "Thank you." He kissed her cheeks, then her lips. "Thank you for taking care of me."

"And I will do so for the rest of our lives." She left the room feeling confident and he headed to the water closet to shower.

Tomorrow, Vanity Devons would be Wilhelmina Strathmore, the future Duchess of Glastonbury.

{10} I now pronounce you...

S unday passed swiftly as many of the family stopped in to formally meet the Duke of Strathmore, talk about his businesses, and be nosey. He took it all in stride and seemed to enjoy the afternoon. David Sr. fired up the grills and talked shop with Nigel, and of course, fishing. As the hours waned, so did members of the family. In a quiet moment before the setting of the November sun, The Duke stood beside Elena Devonshire with a cup of tea, "Madam, you have said very little since my arrival." He paused and waited for her to say something to him.

Elena Devonshire was a straightforward woman who seldom pulled any punches, "I can only assume that your desire to have her as your wife is about something deeper than the physical to make you board a plane."

Nigel sat the tea cup on the counter top, "I sincerely believe in my heart that what we have transcends the physical. Her beauty is a plus, but her mind is what stole my heart. She is a rare woman and I am a lucky man. I will take great care of your daughter."

Elena placed a perfectly manicured hand upon his arm. But there was something bugging Nigel about her reaction to him and he was compelled to ask, "You seemed to be unsurprised by all of this Madam. It was almost as if you knew..."

"Come with me," was all she said as she led him to the family room. From a glass cabinet, she removed a black photo album and set it upon the large oak desk. It had been a while since the book was opened and Nigel could hear the leather in the spine creak as the cover was flipped open. Elena folded open several pages before she stopped at the one she was searching for, murmuring, "Ahh, here we are."

He could not hide his surprise when she pulled out the black and white photo and handed it to him. "I knew who you were because you look just like your father."

In the photo was a young version of his father, his mother, his aunt, and a hauntingly beautiful young Elena dos Santos Gonçalves. She removed the photo from his hand and put it back in the book. "Your mother and I went to boarding school together. This is when she first met your father, a young Duke, who immediately fell in love with her and moved heaven and earth to be with her."

"I guess it is a small world after all," Nigel said as he gazed at the other photos of his parents and soon-to-be mother-in-law.

"My question to you is, how are you able to do this... I mean marry an American and not be disinherited or lose your titles?"

He took a casual stand with his hands in his pockets as she explained to Elena, "With the birth of George of Cambridge, I am no longer in line for the throne. It helped greatly when William married a commoner which freed many of us to marry whom we wished."

Elena knew better. "Yes, but for your family line, how is this acceptable to your family?" It was her tactful way of asking how his family was going to treat her daughter of a mixed race.

"From my understanding, as long as she is of noble blood, there will be no problem," he eyed Elena with more than a mild curiosity. "I would love to one day hear your story."

It was the first time he had seen her smile and her eyes danced with mischief. "It is said that well-behaved women seldom make history. Open a history book. My story starts there..." She said no more as she led him back to the patio where Vanity nervously awaited his return.

"Everything go okay in there?" Vanity asked Nigel. He only winked as her father called him over.

David Sr. was excited to see Nigel come back to the porch. "Nigel, tell me some more about this yacht. Elena, I am going fishing off the back of his yacht in the Mediterranean!"

Cookie stood next to Vanity, watching her Uncle and Willie's Loverman. Vanity looked at her cousin and told her, "It seems I have been sold for a fishing trip on a yacht."

"But at least you get out of the kitchen and get to be in love," Cookie said as she went back in the house.

When Nigel finally managed to skirt away from the fishing chatter, he made his way to Vanity's side. She was seated in a large Papasan chair where he joined her as she seeded tempting ideas in his head about the plane ride in the morning. "You know, I think I am going to like this whole dating thing with you."

Blue eyes met hers with a feint interest, "And why is that Darling?"

"I am looking forward to making out with you tomorrow... in the car on the way to the airport." She squeezed his thigh. "In the privacy of the plane... we finally get to really touch each other..."

"Goodnight," she told him as she planted a feathery light kiss upon his lips that lingered as she flicked her tongue between his lips. It was a bold move, but a necessary one. It was a taunt to make him long to board the plane right now just so they could be alone.

HE WAS UP EARLY, DRESSED and having a cup of tea with Cookie when she arrived downstairs. His eyes were bright and he greeted her with a kiss, holding her so closely it seemed as if she could feel the beating of his heart through his clothing. He wanted to be alone with her, if for no other reason than to allow his hands some freedom to move from her waist to other parts of her body.

Her phone chirped. Their car had arrived. Elena and David Sr. stood in the living room to wish them a safe journey. Elena hugged her daughter closely whispering in her ear, "trust, let go, and be happy."

She kissed her on the cheek and passed her to David Sr. who swallowed her in a bear hug.

"I love you Daddy." His eyes were brimming with tears as he released her, still holding one of her hands as he shook Nigel's.

David Sr. took his daughter's left hand and placed it in Nigel's, telling him, "You take care of my Baby."

Nigel nodded his consent to her father before planting a quick kiss on Elena's cheek, and they were out the door.

It was only a twenty-minute ride to the airfield from her parent's home, but the two were lip-locked from the moment the driver closed the door. They smooched like teenagers until they arrived at the airfield where Finley and Chuck were waiting to assist the driver with loading their bags.

Vanity was super cheerful as she greeted Chuck, who stood dumbfounded at her friendliness. "I will see you next week in New York, okay?"

She grabbed him and hugged him tight. Chuck only gawked as he watched in amazement at the transformation in her demeanor.

Finley was equally shocked by Nigel, who shook Chuck's hand, thanked him for the hospitality he showed to Finley, and said, "I look forward to reciprocating when you hop over the pond." Nigel headed towards the plane and reached his hand back to grab hold of his bride-to-be. No medication, no cold sweats, no terrors before boarding the plane. Chuck boarded briefly to secure Vanity's rolling cooler. The happy couple barely noticed him as he left the aircraft and Finley secured the doors.

There was no word from the two as Finley taxied the plane, received his clearance, and took flight. Nigel felt like a naughty school boy as he kissed Vanity, allowing his hand to run down her thigh. Vanity was equally happy as her fingers trailed across his chest. An hour later, they were landing in Vegas and Nigel could not stop grinning. Finley asked if they wanted to disembark as he secured the plane, but Nigel said, "I need you to stand at my side as a citizen of the Crown."

As the plane was "parked" and secured, the lip-lock love fest ended. "Well, my darling, it is time for us to be married," Nigel told Vanity.

Finley opened the door and Vanity and Nigel stepped outside the plane to be greeted by a short African American woman with a natural hairdo and very tall, very flamboyant Latino man wearing a string of pearls. "Nigel, Finley," Vanity said as she walked toward to the two, "this is my assistant Jessica and Clarke, Stylist Extraordinaire."

Jessica and Clarke both curtsied, and Finley's eyebrows shot up. He also attempted to raise his hand to point out that men did not curtsey, but Nigel grabbed his wrist. Vanity tried not to laugh, instead focusing her attention on Jessica, who immediately started listing information from a tablet as she ushered the three of them to towards the limo.

It could not be said by anyone that Jessica Malone was not the world's best assistant. A certain skill set is required when dealing with a different lifestyle. Vanity Devons lived a very different life and Nigel was about to find out first-hand. The petite woman wore a cordless headset that she used to communicate with the driver. Once the car doors closed, Jessica went to work.

"The chapel been reserved, we are T-Minus ten on arrival, the property is prepared for your stay, and the fridge has been stocked. You will have use of a town car with a driver for your day of fun," Jessica called out.

She handed Vanity a set of keys. "Finley, Clarke, and I will reside on the second floor, and you and the Duke will have the entire third floor."

Nigel's brows went up and he looked at Finley, who looked back at him with his mouth opened. Finley's eyebrows had not come down, especially when Clarke opened what looked like a purse and begin to spritz and prep Vanity. Jessica's phone chirped and she hit the button, "Go!"

The car begins to move. Vanity seemed nonplussed at the hectic pace of it all, as Jessica continued, "Your Grace, for today's activities, Clarke will redress the two of you as American tourists. Finley, you will be with us, and we will show you the city."

She never broke character or pace, "Vanity, lunch will be removed from the cooler and placed in a smaller container for portability. Dinner will be ready at the house for the two of you at 6 pm sharp." Jessica handed Vanity the tablet to check the schedule.

Vanity checked the electronic scheduler, made a couple of swipes, and handed it back. Clarke remained quiet the entire time, only adding more gloss to Vanity's lips. "Tomorrow's activities will begin at noon with a photo shoot. Your Grace, you will receive some media training from Clarke before an early afternoon tea. Your dinner will be served promptly at 6 pm before the actual event at 8 pm. I told them to expect your arrival at 9:05." Vanity held onto Nigel's hand as she looked at him and smiled. He smiled back, lost in his thoughts.

I got on a plane without sedation.

Jessica was not fazed by the romance in the air. "Vanity, LAX nightclub in the Luxor has sent a check for $50,000 if you will make an appearance. The Chateau has offered you $75,000 if you stop in and say a few words and do a photo op with the owner," Jessica said, locking up briefly.

Vanity asked, "What about the Wynn?"

With a few clicks of her rubber tipped pen across the screen, "It appears that GaGa will be at XS and Jermaine Dupree will be at the Encore Beach Club."

As Nigel watched her face, the wheels were turning in her mind, planning something clever.

She arched a perfectly sculpted eyebrow at Nigel. "Jessica, send out a press release that I am in Vegas and stopping by Tryst with a very special VIP. Work it into the schedule and call TMZ on the burner and mention my arrival with a very special man in my life. Clarke, I will need to do a presto change after I leave the Jean Marc event."

Finley had managed to find his voice, "I'm sorry Ms. Devons, but am I to understand these night clubs will pay you to stop in and have a drink?"

Nigel was still in his own world, sitting in the car smiling. Lost in his thoughts, he went over in his mind: I got on a plane. I am about to marry her. Pretty. Smart. Mine. Wife.

"Yes, I can up the price by choosing where I show up and doing the pre-press for the venue. Now, there will be crowds outside to get a peek at me in person. Most people think that I am cosmetically or surgically enhanced, so appearing now and then in person with little to no makeup is free hot press for the night clubs," Vanity told him. Jessica, who had been typing away on the tablet, leaned across the seat and closed Finley's mouth with the tip of her stylus.

She continued talking as if nothing was amiss, "We are out the door tomorrow by 11 pm and Finley, we will need wheels up by 11:30 pm. Please spend much of the day tomorrow sleeping as we will be flying all night."

Finley nodded. Jessica added, "We will arrive back in New York at 6:30 am, in time for a light breakfast. Your Wednesday meetings have been canceled to give you the day with your husband, and Thursday morning there are four meetings back to back because of the reschedule." Jessica finally looked up from the tablet and she clicked the earpiece, "We are T-Minus two minutes. Are there any questions?"

Jessica reached inside her pocket and handed Vanity a black jewelry box. "Per your specifications, Jakob made what you asked for," she remarked. The limo turned into an alley and the car stopped. Jessica stepped from the car, went inside the building, and came back a few seconds later. She peeped her head inside the door, "Show time."

Vanity and Nigel climbed out of the car and walked into the chapel. Jessica presented documents that had been prepared by Khalea to the Chaplain. From nowhere, Clarke plopped a veil on her head and boutonnieres on Finley and Nigel's lapels. Jessica pushed Nigel and Vanity forward, placed Finley at Nigel's side, and she stood beside Vanity. Clarke added a small bouquet of Gerber daisies to Vanity's hands and the wedding began. The entire ceremony lasted less than five minutes.

Nigel said his vows and added a diamond-encrusted band to Vanity's left hand, and she placed a sapphire-studded silver band on his left ring finger. Jessica ushered them back to the car and soon they were underway to the rented house.

Finley looked at Nigel. Still amazed that one could get married so quickly in America. His boss, was still zoned out and in a world all of his own, with an affixed grin plastered to his face. Vanity wasn't far behind him. She was truly happy and soon the world would know, that Vanity Devons was now married.

{11} Presenting Mr. & Mrs....

Clarke helped the driver unload the bags, tipped him, and sent him on his way as they reached the rented space that would be home for the next 27 hours. Seven minutes later, a black town car arrived and instructions were given to the driver to pull into the garage and wait by the service elevator. When they entered the house, everything was the same color and Nigel blinked several times to adjust his eyes to all the beige. Jessica handed them both small bottles of water with a command to "Drink please," as she led them to the elevator. She pointed toward the kitchen and the dining area that would be converted for media training and photos for tomorrow. When the elevator reached the second floor, she gave a gentle nudge to Finley as the three of them exited the lift.

The third floor was the last stop and Vanity and Nigel stepped into a big space with a king-sized bed in the middle of the room, two large side doors, and in the corner, a sitting area with a television and desk. This room was all white. Nigel was frowning. He hated this room. *I got on a plane for this?*

A loud buzz filled the cavernous white space as Vanity made her way to the wall to press a button that opened the elevator doors. Clarke entered with a hanging bag for each of the newlyweds. "Your Grace, your dressing area is to the left," he said, handing him a bag and pointing.

Vanity knew the drill. She took hers and headed to her dressing area, changed quickly into the pink scuffed-up Keds, a pair of sweat pants, and a pink and white tee with a green strawberry in the middle. As she stepped from the room, Clarke clipped a fanny pack around her waist and slipped a clear green visor on her head as he prepared a coil of her braid on the back of her head with butterfly hair clips. A pair of strawberry earrings was now bobbing from her ears, and he applied a layer of truly greasy lip gloss with shades slipped into the cleavage of her tee. Her look was complete.

Nigel not only hated the room, but truly detested what Clarke had given him to wear. The dungarees were saggy, the belt was worn, and the tee shirt was not fit to be worn to clean his stables. It was a Rolling Stones shirt with just the red tongue sticking out. The shoes were the unfamiliar form of a trainer with no real support, even though they covered his ankles. Clarke removed his Jaeger-LeCoultre watch and replaced it with a Timex with a plastic band. Vanity tried her best to stifle her laughter as Clarke added a camera around his neck and a blue baseball cap with the flag of Great Britain embroidered above the bib.

She held out her hand for him to take, but Nigel shook his head no. Her laughter rang out and filled the white space as she grabbed hold of his hand and pulled him toward the elevator. Jessica was waiting inside and pushed B as they headed to the garage to meet the town car and spoke briefly with the driver before handing them both burner phones.

She spoke in the same droll tone, "I have taken your phones so that you will not be tempted to make or take any calls during your day of nuptial sightseeing. These have been programmed with all important numbers, including both your respective parents, and the driver." She handed a phone to Nigel, "and Finley for you."

She handed the second phone to Vanity, "Both of course have my number programmed into it."

Jessica opened the car door and Vanity slid in with Nigel following suit. "It is 11 am. We will see you back here at 5:45." She loaded in the lunch cooler and closed the door. The driver pulled away and Nigel sat staring her with his mouth opened. She started to laugh.

"Bloody hell!" he said as he looked at her incredulously, "What the bollocks just happened and what am I bloody wearing?"

She laughed harder. He held up his foot, "What the bloody hell are these things that are offending my feet?"

"These are called Converse, Chuck Taylor editions," she held back the laughter.

He did not miss a beat, "Well, I need to converse with Mr. Taylor about his taste."

She moved closer to him, "Nigel, today we are your average American couple on honeymoon in Vegas. We are supposed to blend in and be incognito, like undercover or something."

"Undercover as what, the village idiots?" He tugged at the seat of his baggy jeans, "I think I lost my twig and berries in these pants!"

She fell over in the seat, her body racked with laughter. He touched the fanny pack, "And what in the bollocks is this supposed to be?"

She explained to him the many uses for the fanny pack, opening it to pull out wet wipes, hand sanitizer, the atrocious lip glosser she was wearing, and a few loose bills. "I think Clarke replaced the pounds in your wallet with some American dollars," she said as she snuggled close to him, wrapping her arms about his waist.

"Dear Jesus in Heaven," was all he said as she inched closer and convinced him he needed to check the wear ability of this lip gloss.

The afternoon of honeymoon fun was an entire blast and the laughter continued. Vanity felt the most priceless moment occur when they stood in front of the Bellagio watching the water show. She pointed for Nigel to look to his left where an Asian man was wearing the identical outfit, including the camera. To his right, a young white male was wearing a similar outfit with a brown tee that said Lynyrd Skynyrd. The young man looked at Nigel and said, "Duuuude!"

Nigel mouthed to her, "Kill me."

They ventured low and high to the top of the Stratosphere hotel, then over to the MGM Grand to a watching the feeding of the lions, and last a quick hop over to Treasure Island to see the Mutiny on the Bounty. They had two hours to spare and she wanted to head to the Freemont experience. Their stay did not last long when someone recognized her and wanted a photo. She pretended not to speak English and lapsed into Portuguese to ward the fan away, but he was insistent and Nigel stepped in to be her hero.

She was impressed, but the young man was with a group, and things could go really wrong, really fast, so she pulled Nigel by the arm, speed dialed their ride that met them at the corner, and they headed back to the rental house.

INSTINCT TOLD HER TO take the elevator all the way up to the third floor and head to the bedroom to change for dinner; Nigel followed along without question. In her dressing closet, she was pleased at Clarke's selection of attire for the evening and thought Nigel would be wowed. Tonight, she would release the braid and let the hair hang freely down her back. She popped in the shower and was feeling tingly about her evening.

NIGEL ENTERED HIS CLOSET to find on a male mannequin his attire for the evening. It was a combination of his clothing and a few new pieces. It was definitely his jacket but the brocaded waist coat was a snazzy burgundy color with blue faux gemstone blue buttons. The blue shirt with burgundy cuffs and collar were pretty sharp. He actually forgave Clarke for the earlier shoe disaster when he looked down and saw the beautiful shoes he had put with the ensemble. He peered outside the door to see if his wife was watching. He hopped in the shower and made quick work of his routine while his stomach reminded him that lunch was a bit light, and he was famished.

Husband and wife excited their dressing rooms at the same time. Vanity looked impeccable in a strapless off-white satin tulle princess-style A-line ankle-length wedding dress with a burgundy lace sash. Her hair was hanging freely down her back and she had added a pop of color to her lips. Nigel's breath caught when he saw her standing there. My wife. He looked at his left hand to eye the blue sapphire band. I am married. He considered himself the luckiest man in the world to have such a stunning creature at his side. He extended his arm, "Shall we, my Dear? I am rather famished."

They took the stairs, only to find a trail of rose petals at the bottom. The photos they had taken earlier with the digital camera had been framed and were sitting about the foyer on the credenza. Nigel did not remember sitting the camera down in a common area, but Jessica must have gotten hold of it and printed the images from the disk. Vanity smiled as she looked at the photo she had taken of Nigel standing next to his doppelgänger. The happy couple followed the trail of roses to a perfectly set a table for two that rivaled the best table in any restaurant. A waiter materialized from the kitchen to take their orders from the limited menu and Nigel chose the steak with lobster tails and Vanity the grilled chicken and shrimp.

A bottle of champagne was opened and she sipped lightly to the toast to their health. Music from a violinist who also came from the kitchen and began to play, and Nigel rose to ask her to join him in their wedding dance. This was their wedding night and although it would not end in the traditional way, this moment was going to be very special.

The next two hours sped by quickly and the next day was going to be a fourteen hour marathon. Nigel yawned first and looked at her with that smile. She took him by the arm as he led her back to the bedroom.

"I must say," Nigel started, "Your assistant, although a bit scary, is top notch; dinner was amazing." Vanity was tired and fretting about the rest of the night. She could not help but be worried that he may feel that after the morning smooching session, he would want to exercise his husbandly rights. A light squeeze to his arm was her only response.

His only words to her upon entering the bedroom were, "Meet me in the middle," as he pointed to the bed and released her before heading to his dressing area to disrobe. Brush, floss, wash the face, double check the teeth, and eyed himself in the mirror before returning the bed. He was about to head to bed with the most beautiful woman in the world. He was getting everything he asked for minus the sex, but that would come. He promised he would not rush her and he would keep his word.

Clad in boxers and a tee, he slid in between the covers and was happy to find that his side of the bed was firm. Curiosity made him roll to her side which was much softer. It was not possible to stay in the middle because of a dividing partition. She cleared her throat, startling him and he jumped, "I was trying to determine which side of the bed would be mine, I think the firmer side would be more my preference." He said it in the form of a question and he saw the hesitation in her eyes. The buzzer sounded as Vanity opened the elevator doors to let in Clarke, who made quick work of putting her loose hair into a braid. He exited as quietly as he had arrived, leaving the two of them alone.

"I never sleep with it loose. It would be a nightmare. I did once and woke up with a mouthful of it that nearly suffocated me," she told Nigel in an effort to lighten the tension in the room.

Tossing back her side of the covers, he used two fingers to beckon her forward. She was slow to move and he gave her another reassuring smile. "Wilhelmina, do try to keep your hands to yourself and stay on your side of the bed," Nigel said as he pulled the covers up around his neck. Vanity's heart was pounding in her chest, her breasts were tingling, and her girl parts were doing a dance in her pajama shorts. She imagined he was thinking she was afraid he would try something when the opposite was on her mind. Vanity wanted to roll on top of him and rub her body against his until the tingling stopped.

She inhaled, exhaled, and slid in between the covers. He was so warm. His legs were hairy and he smelled even better half-dressed than he did in the sexy suit he wore earlier tonight. Her body was rigid when he leaned over with his lips puckered. She kissed them and he rolled to his side, slipped his hand into hers and was ready to rest his mind after saying "See you in the morning, Mrs. Strathmore."

"Good night, Nigel."

The lights were turned off and he whispered her name.

"Yes, Nigel?"

"I got on a plane today..."

"You did great Mr. Strathmore," were her soft words into the darkened chamber.

She felt his warm breath when he breathed deep and exhaled, and soon he was sleeping. Vanity lay next to him wide awake, feeling out of sorts and wanton for wanting him to touch her in the worst way and wanting him more than she had ever wanted anything in her life.

The woman in Vanity Devons was coming awake.

{12} Say Cheese...

The sound of the television woke Nigel with a start and he was a bit confused trying to remember where he was. His wife was no longer in bed but the scent of her still remained on the pillow which gave him raging morning wood, and he headed towards the bathroom to splash cold water on his face to calm down. He looked at himself in the mirror, trying to remember the last time he was actually with a woman. He spent so much time working that he had little time for a social life.

Six months ago... the Italian sales rep? No... she had crazy eyes and was too overzealous. Nine months... the perky red head? No... she was a bloody nutter. Standing in the mirror it came to him that it had been nearly a year since he had been intimate with a woman. Wow! You work too much, old boy.

Calmer now, Nigel took soft steps as he headed toward the sitting area. The television was showing a woman doing yoga and in the middle of the floor was his wife. Nigel was awed to see her legs folded in a lotus position as she balanced herself on her elbows. The amount of discipline it took to master that move required years of training in Yoga. It took breath control and emotional control. Her muscles were well trained and did not strain as she maneuvered from a crow, to a limited half crow, and into a firefly pose. Wilhelmina was always in control of her emotions, her facial expressions, and by the look of this, she was also in control of her body.

An idea popped into his mind that he believed was brilliant. He went back to the bed and waited for his wife to come and wake him.

THE WAIT FOR HIS WIFE'S return to their sleeping area was short and she rounded his side of the bed and gently stroked his cheek, "Time for school." It was an old trick her mother had taught her to keep from scaring the crap out of a sleeper, especially her brother. Nigel stretched, slowly turning and wishing her a good morning.

"We have a fourteen-hour day today, so you must hydrate and monitor your sodium intake. Let's get ready for breakfast." Her words were softly spoken which made him feel bad for what he was about to do, but he wanted...needed her...to need him. Nigel threw back the covers and stood up with a deep stretch. In one motion, he removed his tee while asking his wife, "Is there someone to handle my dirty bits, or do I wait to we get back to your place tomorrow?"

Vanity's eyed his hairy chest, watching the trail of hair that disappeared into his boxers. A mumbled answer was all he received as he removed the boxers while he entered his bathroom, just showing her enough of his backside as he started the shower, washing longer than usual to give his wife time to complete her grooming. Still wet and draped only in a towel, he left his bathroom to find her. "Darling, what should I wear today, or is Clarke going to style me?"

Vanity turned to see her husband standing before her looking like a cold bottle of water on a hot day. "Nigel!" she exclaimed, "You are almost naked!"

He gave her a reassuring smile and removed the towel, handing it to her. "Darling, I am your husband. You will see me naked often."

Her eyes grew wide as they followed the hair trail from his chest to his navel, watching it narrow at his belly button and expand to a triangle right around his.. "Ooh that's nice!"

Her hand was extending to try to poke it with her finger, but Nigel grabbed the wayward digit, "Wilhelmina, my eyes are up here.'"

Prying her eyes away from what she imagined being a good time, she shook her head to regain her focus, "Yes, so sorry. Just put on some loungers with a tee for breakfast and everything else will be downstairs."

Nigel was really rubbing the moment in and embraced her fully with a soft kiss on her mouth, "I'm excited to spend a day in your world."

She watched his naked bum walk away.

"Dang it," was all she could say.

Nigel had made a strategic move and had planted the seed. The only thing he needed was just needed a bit of miracle growth solution and their marriage would come to fruition.

THE MORNING WAS A WHIRLWIND after breakfast. Nigel was prod-ded, poked, twisted, and posed in several suits. Wilhelmina looked lovely in a white gown with soft blue trimming as they took pictures on the stair well and in the foyer and playful photos in the kitchen.

"Your Grace," Clarke called to him. "There will be several photo opportu-nities this afternoon."

Vanity stood next to Clarke and hit her trademark pose.

Clarke told Nigel, pointing to his boss, "This is her trademark stance."

Her right leg was extended with her ankle turned slightly outwards, her face at a 45-degree angle. Vanity shifted the position to her left side.

Clarke went on, "This is her second pose which is utilized if she has to be shot from her left side." In two moves, the Duke was shown where to stand with his wife and hand placement for the shot.

"Our money shot for this evening will be a left side pose with the wedding rings on your shoulder," Clarke told Nigel as he stepped in front of Vanity and struck the pose. "Every shot you take tonight will be in this framework."

"Got it," Nigel said.

Jessica entered the room with a cell phone in hand, "Vanity, I have Mr. Wynz on the line for you."

She excused herself from the exercise as Clarke continued showing Nigel his best angles for taking photos. He snapped photos of Nigel. Immediately showing him the images, the angles in the frame. He practiced intense eyes and smiling eyes poses and Nigel could not wait to escape.

"Good morning Jeb. How are you?" Vanity said into the phone. Nigel tried to listen in, but was uncertain of what he was hearing. "If I crash the other two functions that will cost you more. I am willing to stay a half hour, have one drink, and do three photos for a hundred."

The voice on the other line must not have been pleased. "Not a problem, but I wanted to give you first dibs. The guest I am bringing is a very special VIP and it will make world news for at least two weeks. Three photos in front of your logo will be front and center on every news outlet."

Vanity looked at Nigel and winked before returning to the call, "A photo with you, me and the VIP will cost you an extra 25, but I look forward to seeing you tonight." The phone was handed back to Jessica. "Will you please adjust the schedule by twenty minutes?"

The time flew by and before long it was time to get dressed and head out the door. Nigel was amazed at the transformation by his wife Wilhelmina into the larger-than-life Vanity Devons. Clarke was amazing as he styled her hair, but mid-way through the process, his wife took a look at herself in the mirror and stopped everything.

"This look is all wrong. The first image the Duchess of Strathmore will see of me will be this photo. I will not be introduced to the world as his wife looking like I just stepped out of Studio 54," she said as she went through the rack of clothing that Clarke had brought in. Vanity also eyed the selection for Nigel for the evening.

"Wrong, wrong, and wrong," she said as she checked the clothing options. "He should be photographed tonight wearing a British designer. Anything he wears in New York will be an American designer." The clothes Nigel held in his hand, she took away and handed back to Clarke. "Get on the phone if you must, but dress us in something befitting his title, please Clarke."

Forty-five minutes later, dressed, looking fantastic, and ready to head out for the night, Nigel watched Jessica strap on the ear piece and start clicking at the pad. He eyed his wife, who had transformed from the sweet woman in a car terrified of intimacy to a woman of the world who wielded her power.

Out of curiosity he asked, "What is our ETA, Jessica?"

"We are at T-15 seconds. Places please," she called out. Vanity wore black palazzo pants with a soft white silk blouse and a bright red belt. Nigel was dressed in a Paul Smith black suit with a white waistcoat and a red tie. Inside the limo, she placed her hand upon his and told him, "The lights will be bright, but focus on me Nigel." She was concerned because he seemed out of sorts.

"Are you okay?"

He looked down at his clothing. What he was wearing was not of his choosing, but to his liking. "I have only been married for a day or so and I am concerned if I will ever be able to dress myself again," he said with a straight face.

"Don't worry, you are in good hands," she said as Jessica called out the two second warning.

"Here we go, husband," she told him as the car came to a stop. When the door opened, Nigel swore his heart had as well. His wife, Vanity Devons was going to work.

The flash of the cameras nearly blinded Nigel as he stepped from the car. Vanity held his hand as they walked the gauntlet of people yelling out her name, "Vanity, over here!"

"Vanity! Vanity!"

She paused on the red carpet and posed. Nigel remembered his training from the morning. If she poses with the right leg, I step left. Left leg, I stand right. Behind her, hand on top of hers, don't cover the rings.

"Vanity who is the mystery man?" someone yelled out. With grace and elegance, Vanity stopped in front of the Wynn Hotel logo, slowly raised her left hand against her right cheek with the wedding rings facing the camera as if she were whispering a secret.

"Mystery Man?" She said with feigned amusement, "he is my husband."

Vanity held the pose for a few seconds allowing the photogs to snap the picture of the rings.

It took everything in Nigel not to jump when every camera went off at once. Bulbs were flashing, people were yelling her name, and someone even yelled his, but he remained poised as they went inside the new Jean Marc Salon. His composure did not last when a 6-foot burly black man with blonde bouffant hair and a pink ponytail sashayed over to them yelling, "Vanity, you delicious vixen! You didn't tell me you got married. Is this him?"

"Yes, you overly dramatic queen. This is my husband Nigel Strathmore," she told the over exuberant hair dresser.

"Dang girl, he is a fine-looking some- some. Can I touch him?" Jean Marc asked, and Vanity was surprised when Nigel responded.

"No, you may not. If you like the feel of what you are touching, you may try to keep me," he stared at John Marc with eyes so blue that the hairdresser's knees physically buckled.

"Dear Lawd, I think I just came," John Marc said with a bit too much sass as he fanned himself with pink polished fingernails, but Nigel was having fun.

"If that is all it takes, then touching me would ruin you and that pink polish for the rest of the week," he said, slipping his arm about Vanity's waist. "Darling, I do believe I am in need of that drink."

"And a sexy British accent, too. Lawd, let me touch him, just once!" Jean Marc yelled at the back of Nigel's head. Nigel held up his finger wagging it at Jean Marc, "Behave yourself," he told him and winked with a smile.

It set a lighthearted mood for the next fifteen minutes, which is what Jean Marc knew he was only going to get from his first and most famous customer. He had come a long way since her brother David had hired him fresh out of beauty school and he had her to thank for half of his success. The business was booming with her as a co-owner, and she never missed a milestone in his life or a ribbon-cutting ceremony. She even remembered to send him a personally signed birthday card and a present every year.

After cutting the ribbon and pouring champagne to celebrate the new opening, she and Nigel slipped out the side entrance down a back hall and exited a side door down the walkway from the nightclub Tryst. Jessica was already in place along with the media as they walked side by side down the corridor through the throng of reporters and lookee-loos.

Jessica, as part of the crowd, yelled out, "OMG, it's Vanity Devons!"

This spurred a maelstrom of camera phones recording and snapping pics. Vanity stopped in front of the signage of the club to pose for candid photos of her and Nigel. This time she faced Nigel with the wedding rings prominently displayed on his shoulder.

The hotel owner made his appearance, ushered them into the club, and had a celebratory bottle of champagne sent over, but Vanity asked for it not to be opened. It did not take Jeb long to break the ice, "And who is the mystery man, Vanity?"

She was almost like a cat with a mouthful of a canary. "This is Nigel Strathmore, the fourth Duke of Glastonbury, the Earl of Strathmore and the owner of Strathmore Textiles."

It was worth the wait to see Jeb's mouth drop, "But I heard he didn't fly! How long has he been in America?" He turned to Nigel, suddenly remembering his manners. "How long are you staying Your Grace?"

It was Nigel's turn to get in on the fun. "Until my wife tells me it is time to head home."

He looked at Vanity and leaned forward. She took his cue and met him halfway, connecting her lips to his and bringing her left hand up to his face. Cameras flashed and clicked as reporters all ran to be the first to break the story.

In the morning the world would know the Duke of Glastonbury was in America and married to Vanity Devons.

{13] Welcome Home...

On the ride from the hotel to the airstrip, Nigel could see the mental transition his wife was making from her public persona back to the role of the woman who would share his life. He watched with an interest in the limo as Clarke removed the fake lashes and light makeup. As they arrived at the airfield, the same red cooler from a few days before was loaded into the plane.

What is in the cooler?

Somewhere between the times they had taken off in Phoenix and reloading in Vegas, the interior of his plane had been modified. A black privacy drape had been added between the front seats and the rear seats. "I thought we could use some privacy," she told him and she dropped her pants and removed the white blouse and handed them both to Clarke. He was shocked that she was not wearing the frilly laced panties she designed and sold, but black cotton briefs. Finley was already in the cockpit of the plane firing up the engines.

Out of courtesy, Nigel averted his eyes as she dressed, but as soon as she was dressed and Jessica and Clarke were seated, she whispered in his ear, "You know you will see me naked often. I am your wife." She wiggled her brows at him, "Come, hold me and tell me more about this grand romantic plan of yours." As they taxied down the runway, she began to plant small kisses on his face, then his lips, allowing her tongue to mate with his as she distracted him from the take-off.

The plane landed at 6:30 in the morning, right on time. The deep reclining seats on the plane made it easy to sleep and Vanity had snuggled up in Nigel's embrace as they flew through the night from Las Vegas to Teterboro Airport near the Meadowlands. It was only a twelve-mile drive to midtown Manhattan to her building in the meatpacking district.

There was no mistaking the warmth that emanated from him, and her mind started to wonder how it would feel to have his weight upon her. Finley was a far more skilled pilot than her cousin Chuck and the landing was smooth, barely waking Nigel as Finley put wheels on the tarmac. The curtains between their space and her assistants were closed and she wanted a moment alone with her husband. They would be heading to her home and would have about four days to be together with few if any interruptions at night. She needed to know what his plans were, so she would know whether to be on guard, on defense, or need to sleep in another room.

Gently stroking his face, she spoke softly in his ear, "Nigel, it's time for school." He stirred to find her staring at him, "Welcome to New York." She informed him they had landed and expressed her joy to welcome him and show him her city and their New York home. His hands went to his mouth and she handed him a small dry brush for his teeth which he quickly put to use. Nature was calling on two fronts, pulling Nigel to the loo, but the moment he rose from his seat, his wife noticed the obvious, her eyes wide with concern.

"Nigel, are you..." she paused eyeballing the firmness of his twig and imagining the fullness of his berries, "hmm, hungry?"

Confused, he looked at his stomach to see if maybe she had heard it rumble then he noticed his state. Afraid and very hesitant to answer for fear that he did not truly understand the question, it also let him know that she did not understand a man's body even though she spent a great deal of time with her two brothers. An arched brow was all he could muster at this point any way.

I just flew across America. Again. In a plane. Probably over some water.

His head was swimming with thoughts. It was 6:30 in the morning, his bladder was full, and he had a raging woody that caused his beautiful wife obvious trepidation.

"When my brothers are in need of some time with a woman," she lowered her eyes away from him, "they say they are hungry." She pointed to the bulge in his pants, "Are you hungry, Nigel?"

His answer was a smile, along with the words, "I can't be." He helped her to her feet to stand toe to toe with him, her hazel eyes beseeching his blue ones, "I can only sate my appetite when my wife is ready to feed me."

The look of relief on her face was palpable. There were things which needed to be addressed between them before they left the plane. She needed to know he would not rush her, but he needed to know she wasn't going to make him wait forever. A compromise was required.

"Wilhelmina, might I have a moment?" He touched her chin with his forefinger, "A slight liberty, or a nibble if you will."

Her agreement yielded his hands to her waist as he angled her body and pulled her close to him where his need was pressed at the juncture between her thighs. He did not rub, grind, and grope at her. Instead his words were soft as he explained, "Together we will learn how to feed each other." His words softly whispered, "I am excited to learn things that please you. I am eager to teach you the things that please me." He planted a small kiss on her jawline.

"I can't wait to enjoy our hours together as we teach each other." His lips grazed her neck as he continued to explain that there were non-invasive techniques, they could employ to enjoy each other. "I have so much to show you, so much about you I want and need to learn." Another nibble at her neck and she found herself pressing closer to him, "You are my wife, my love, the woman with whom I will share the rest of my life." She threw her arms around his neck and held him close.

"I will give you all the time you need to get to know me and, I you," he said in her ear. Deep down, he wanted to let her know that he was anxious for her to share his bed, but he didn't want to come across as a man who was eager for her to serve as fodder his libido. "Each minute we spend together is special, dressed or undressed, Wilhelmina," his lips found hers, "you feed my soul."

The kiss was deep, passionate, and all-inclusive. The feel of him against her was causing havoc on her hormones and she was ready to allow him to have his way with her. They heard the clearing of a throat and slowing pried themselves apart.

"Your Grace, Vanity, the cars have arrived. We must depart," Jessica announced.

Nigel still held his wife close, never looking over his shoulder or letting her go as he spoke to the assistant, "Give us a moment please, Jessica, if you will."

Still holding each other, they both exhaled as Nigel whispered in her ear, "Damn, you feel so amazing in my arms."

Vanity Devons was not a woman to curse, but in her mind, she had just become a sailor. Her husband's body felt amazing against hers as well and it was going to be a battle to be a lady and wait to get to know him.

Vanity Devon's body wanted to know him right now.

{14} How you living...

The limo drove down Hudson, making a right onto Jane, swinging back around to Horatio and stopping in front of a plain brick building with large windows on the fourth floor. During the twelve-mile ride, Jessica said very little other than to hand her boss and the Duke a yogurt and a banana to start the morning. She remained quiet when Vanity's phone rang, but the familiar ringtone was from her twin brother. It was unusual not to speak with him every day and even more so for him not to have been at her side for her wedding, but she understood. He was on a honeymoon.

The call was brief. He and Elsie had departed Puerto Rico, spent a few nights in Miami, and were headed her way. They were landing in an hour and wanted to spend a night with her and his new brother-in-law. She looked at Nigel, but there was nothing to say. Will was in route. The call ended. And she updated everyone in the car and asked Jessica to make sure Phan picked up pork chops for dinner.

Nigel assumed that Phan was the housekeeper and since his wife had not chosen to elaborate on the subject, he did not make a mention of it either as they headed towards her home. Jessica pulled two envelopes from her tablet cover, handing one to Vanity and the other to the Duke, "As you requested Vanity."

Uncertain of what was in the envelope, Nigel opened it to find a check for $75,000. His eyes were wide, but Vanity only leaned in and kissed his cheek. "That's your half of the earnings from last night."

He sat dumbfounded. I didn't do anything but stand there. The world his wife lived in was very different from his own and he had a lot to learn in a few days. Nigel Strathmore looked forward to ever moment.

THE BUILDING IN WHICH Vanity resided was a plain brick four story on the lower east side of the Hudson River. The limo stopped at the front door and Vanity climbed out, dragging Nigel with her. The car continued on around the block. The front of the building held no windows, just a large VP on the side of the structure with the signature bird logo. The left side of the building had a paned glass window which read, "Marzetti & Associates."

Nigel stared at the name. It sounded familiar. Vanity answered the question on his face by simple stating, "It's Khalea and her husband Stephano's New York offices."

As they entered the building, Nigel was surprised by how well-lit and bright it was inside compared to the dismal-looking outside. There was a very large reception area with closed caption monitors behind the desk. He noticed on the screen Jessica and Clarke loading luggage into a freight elevator in the rear of the building.

Vanity said, "The first floor is an open meeting space. When Vanity's Pleasure is in full production for a fashion show or a photo shoot, these rooms are used by make-up, hair, editing, retouches, and all those unglamorous things that make models look fabulous."

She continued to explain when they were not in production, the rooms were often leased out to artists, small business owners, and locals who needed a meeting space or a small reception. "This way, the building helps pay for itself." Nigel was impressed.

The elevator behind the receptionist's desk only went to the second floor where her offices were located. "VP is located mainly on the right side of the building, with the back-floor space as a photo area. We have 3200 square feet, the law firm has 1600, and they use the downstairs conference rooms for large meetings, which are rare."

The doors to the offices of Vanity's Pleasure were glass with carved models adorning all but the handles. The lobby was simply decorated with overstuffed red and orange couches and large vases of glass flowers. Over the big sofa was a photo of a young Vanity Devons. The photo was taken at a beach. Vanity's toes were dug in the sand and her arms were wrapped around her knees, her hair flying freely in the wind. A smile came to his lips because her eyes had the same intensity when she was ten as they did today. "That is my favorite photo," Vanity said as she moved closer to the enlarged picture. "This was taken at the Lake House."

Nigel asked if it was the same Lake House from her brother's wedding. "Yes," she smiled a gigantic grin that also made Nigel smile with her. "This one was taken by my dad. He actually has a very good eye and is an amateur photog."

She took him by the hand, telling him, "Let me show you where I work."

There was a small conference room after the lobby which was directly across from the bathrooms. The next office was large, spacious, and meticulously organized. Two chairs sat in front of a wooden desk, and a small window that held fresh flowers had been cracked to allow in morning air. He knew this was Jessica's office.

The next office was slightly larger, with a work table, a sewing machine, four mannequins, and racks of shoes and clothing. This office had to belong to Clarke. The next office was a tad bit larger with a small glass desk, a sewing machine, a drafting table and fabric swatches. It was well lit, with a large window that faced the Hudson, and a large television. It was not at all what he expected.

Across the hall from her office was a break room that had lots of counter space, a Sub-Zero fridge, and a large dining table. The back room held an open space. The right side of the room held a red runway carpet that ended with changing rooms behind the red curtains and was adorned with red cushioned chairs for viewers.

The left side of the room hosted a wall with lights for all sorts for photography. The back wall held a massive green screen. "I save millions each year by shooting on a green screen versus on location. Since most of my lines are one of a kind and custom orders, most of the photos are for catalogue use only." He nodded as they headed out a back door toward the freight elevator heading to the third floor.

The third floor held corporate apartments. Apartment one belong to Jessica and apartment two belonged to Clarke. Three and four were corporate apartments for Marzetti and Associates and the remaining two were efficiencies; one belonged to VP and the other to the firm. "If Finley had opted to stay with you, he would have had use of one of these apartments," Vanity smiled at him, then corrected herself, "or one of these efficiency flats."

Her smile was mesmerizing. Her hazel eyes were alluring. Her mind, sharp, but what he needed to see was her living space. Nigel had severed his relationship with several women because of the way the women lived, which said more about who a woman actually was than the designated representative she sent out in public. Thus far, his beautiful wife was everything he had believed her to be, but the moment of truth was around the corner. He felt himself getting nervous. Did she have a dirty secret that he would have to live with for the rest of his life? This was the one thing in this whole idea of his that frightened him, causing hesitation and dread. Either way, they were now married and he found he was sweating a bit.

His fear was not unfounded. Several years prior, he had dated a model with a hyphenated name that also lived a hyphenated life. It was three weeks before she took him to her place. When he arrived, he was shocked. Every wall was adorned with Herculean-sized photos of her on the cover of magazines. Nigel felt he could have tolerated a bit of narcissism, but there were other things about her that rubbed him wrong.

A firm believer that what you put in your body says a great deal about how you feel about yourself, alarm bells went off in his head when he opened her pantry to find only jars of pickles and olives. The fridge only held small containers of yogurt and bags of celery stalks. The freezer which truly concerned him, only held eight bottles of flavored vodka. The kitchen was only half of the nightmare.

Her bathroom was disgusting and the bedroom had clothing strewn about the place. Many of the items of clothing were designer originals, yet she had little or no regard for the care of the fabric or the designer's hard work. What really set his duff in a dander was when she gave a thousand dollar shoe to her Shit-zu as a chew toy. That was just no way to treat good leather.

Nigel shivered a bit as he thought of the famous British actress that he dated for two months. Katlin's London townhome's walls were covered in mirrors so that she would be able to glance at herself no matter where she sat or stood in any room. In the two months that he dated her, Nigel had gained ten pounds from dining out. She maintained her figure by eating only once a day, and that was only dining on a few leaves of lettuce and a crouton. He, on the other hand, had adopted her eating habit, but by dinnertime he had been starving and would order large meals with dessert. In her townhome, her fridge was littered with takeout boxes, foil wrappers shaped like various fowls, and a weird smell that haunted him to this day.

That could have been worked around, but she often referred to herself in third person, constantly dropping names of celebrities and royalty as if he didn't know who was whom in Great Britain. Kaitlin was surprised when she had been invited to Buckingham Palace and forced him to come along. It never dawned on her that he was the Queen's great nephew and that the Prince Regent was his cousin. All of that aside, he still enjoyed her free flowing attitude that was a direct juxtaposition to his no nonsense persona. It is what he loved about his wife. She brought out his playful side.

A week after he had met Wilhelmina, he ran into Kaitlin at a social function of the Prince Regent. He didn't recognize her. Her face was wracked with signs of Botox and collagen injections, and something was wrong with her lips. It was nonsensical to him. Physical beauty was a plus but a beautiful soul was a must.

The things he felt were important in a wife and a companion had been evident with just three hours in the company of Wilhelmina Devonshire. He had only been in the U.S. for five days and had experienced things in a way that lightened his soul. The real Wilhelmina was about to be revealed as they took the elevator to the fourth floor and entered her living space.

{15] Honey, we're home...

S he opened the loft style sliding door and Nigel's breath caught. "Whoa," was all he could muster. The apartment was a large loft styled flat with lots of high windows that brought in tons of natural light.

"Welcome home, Honey," she said with a smile. The living, common, dining, and kitchen were all in a large bay. The living room was slightly recessed into the floor, but not quite sunken, with a farmhouse style fireplace facing the door. The overstuffed Corinthian leather sofa, with two matching loungers in the softest shades of gray, was adorned with red, sienna and deep orange pillows. Nigel wanted to grab a book from the bookshelf that started on the floor and went all the way to the ceiling and covered the entire wall and was laden with books. He moved closer to the bookshelf and realized it was a library and the books were organized by author and genre. He only stood quietly as he took it all in.

The farmhouse fireplace had an actual cast-iron pot in it, and beside it were marshmallow roasting sticks. He began to imagine cold New York nights with a book, making s'mores and reading to their children. Over the fireplace was a photo that had been printed on canvas of two children running along the water's edge. The children were beautiful, but the look of terror on the little girl's face made him move closer to examine the images. Nigel asked her, "What is that in the little boy's hand?"

Without even looking at the photo, she looked Nigel squarely in the face and told him, "It's a snake."

Nigel's eyes widened, and she went on, "Funny thing is, Daddy took several pictures of Will chasing me with that darn thing before he made him put it down." Nigel looked closer at the photo and his Wilhelmina was truly frightened. Will's face was of sheer joy, chasing her with the snake, and he momentarily envied her relationship with her brother. "Come husband, let me show you the rest of our home," she extended her hand and led him to a large common area.

He immediately noticed the upright piano, the comfortable chairs in red fabric, the big screen television, and a gaming table in the middle of the fray. He really loved this space. He even loved the colorful red, blue, and gray rug that tied the living room colors to this area. The color scheme continued into the dining room.

The dining room table was a slab of gray granite that had been mounted on Mahogany table legs and trimmed around the edges with the same wood. It was clean, smooth and elegant. There was nothing pretentious in the whole space. It was an open bay dining area that seated twelve. On the right side of the room was a built in Mahogany Amish Columbus Buffet Hutch. The cabinet was flush against the wall and had granite that matched the table as a side serving counters and doors underneath. She noticed the look on his face and anticipated his question, "When the family is all here, there are lots of us, and we go through a lot of food."

He turned and looked at the facing wall and there were six black and white photos on the wall. The first he recognized as a younger version of her father with a small boy. David Sr. looked as if he was teaching the boy to fish. Nigel asked, "Is that David in this photo?"

She moved closer, saying, "I hope you were serious when you told my father you fish. He is a bit fanatical about his fishing." He did not respond, but was captured by the next photo of a teenage Wilhelmina getting a make-up lesson from a young and extremely beautiful Elena Devonshire. It was such an intimate moment between mother and daughter. The next photo was of David Sr. with both twins on his lap as he read to them from the Chronicles of Narnia. They were about ten, which was a nice contrast in the next photo of David Sr. reading to all three adult children at the kitchen table. "How old were you in this photo?"

She moved closer, "Will and I are 18 years old in this photo and David is about 27," she paused and looked closer at what he was reading, "Ahh, my father's favorite... Crime and Punishment."

She spoke briefly about the case he was working on at the time that mirrored the story.

"Of course it led to a big argument between the four of us because there is no way that murder is acceptable, even if the needs of many outweigh the needs of a few," she remarked. They entered the kitchen which was bright and sunny and made him want to cook something, even though he had no idea how to cook.

She opened the fridge and he could have sworn he heard angels singing. She was still talking, "I find Dostoyevsky to be a bit heavy handed in his use of symbolism and whipping a horse is just unconscionable." Nigel did not hear a word she said. He was captivated by the order and fullness of the fridge.

There was fresh fruit in individual serving containers, melon slices that he immediately opened and popped a section of Honey Dew into his mouth. He eyed the blueberries, the cheeses, the shelf of bottle water that were labeled VP. Still munching on the fruit, "You bottle your own water?"

"No, we have a filter system on all the water faucets in the building. We recycle the bottles, steam clean them and relabel them with pre-printed labels to reduce the amount of waste." Nigel joined her at the counter and sat on one of the bar stools.

"Oh," he said, "yes, I am an avid fisherman, so I really do fish as often as I can."

Vanity took two small plates from the well-organized cabinet, grabbed a fork, and made her very hungry husband a snack plate of fruits and cheeses. It did not take the kettle long to heat up, and she made him a cup of breakfast tea. She smiled and stopped what she was doing. "Let's finish the tour first, then we will come back here and have a snack." He grabbed a few blueberries and nodded as he followed her down a long hall.

"There are four bedrooms, each with a private," she paused, searching for the right word, "loo."

There was nothing remarkable about the bedrooms. Each room was neat and tastefully decorated and the last bedroom took up the rear of the apartment. As Vanity opened the double doors, she stepped to the side to allow him entry. He was frozen in the doorway.

Above the bed was a photo of the two of them in his tux and her white dress on the night of their wedding. He wasn't sure if it was taken the next day during the photo shoot or the night of the wedding dinner. She looked magnificent. He looked like a man in love.

"Your closet, dressing room, and bathroom are to the left," she told him as she headed towards her closet to change her shoes.

The bedroom was the identical layout as the one in Vegas and included a sitting area with a small floor to ceiling bookshelf that encompassed more design and business books than casual reading. There was a Wii with several Yoga workout CDs and lots of jazz CDs in some sort of surround sound system. Over the television was a photo of the two of them on the roller coaster in Vegas. He laughed at his closed eyes as they went over the drop. Nigel hated roller coasters and was going to burn that photo. He was impressed that Jessica had gotten them developed and hung in less than 48 hours.

Nigel loved the two comfortable chairs and was almost tempted to park himself in one for a moment of respite. He heard her washing her hands again and went to check out his bathroom. He opened the closet to find the clothing from his suitcase had been unpacked, along with some new undergarments that had been placed in the drawers.

Who unpacked my things?

He opened the top drawer to find his watches had been neatly placed, his ties hung, along with his shirts, his jackets, and waistcoats, and he looked for his soiled clothing. Nigel checked his bathroom and fell in love. It had a sauna, a steam shower, a bidet, and a detachable shower head to rinse his berries. He wanted to jump in and wash away the soil of the night travel. He used the loo, washed his hands, and went to test the bed.

Vanity exited her bathroom to find him laid back on the bed. He rolled to his right and then back to his left and shook his head that his side of the bed was just right, but as he rolled back, he noticed the photo on the nightstand.

"No..... no.... no...." Vanity was already laughing. She had been waiting for him to spot the photo of himself in Vegas in the jeans and Chuck Taylor's. Nigel rubbed his eyes, "I wasn't dreaming, was I?"

She shook her head no, and when their eyes met, it was like an instant magnet. He looked at the bed then at her and swung his legs to the side and stood up.

"This is a very big flat for you to live in alone."

She moved closer to him. "I am never alone," she said, and Nigel heard several voices. She placed a light kiss upon his lips as she pulled him by his hands to the kitchen.

Will was in the kitchen with Elsie and the Asian woman from the wedding who had jammed the tampons up his nose.

"I got pork chops for dinner," the Asian woman said as she placed them in the fridge.

Vanity turned to Nigel, "This is our sister Phan."

{16] You did what...

Phan faced Nigel and did a curtsey, "Hello again, your Grace."

Nigel looked confused but smiled, "Well, I am your brother-in-law, so that makes us family." He embraced her, moved to Elsie and kissed both cheeks, and shook Will's hand.

Will told Nigel, "I feel cheated. I didn't get any kisses!"

"I am not Italian. Will, you and I don't ever need to kiss. I don't care how handsome you are," Nigel replied.

Will ribbed Nigel a bit more about him being insensitive to his needs as Vanity took more plates from the cabinet and set out boiled eggs, more blueberries, cheeses, bottles of water, and a small tray of rolled lunch meats. Nigel was looking at Phan, "So what's the story?"

Will's eyes danced as he said, "Willie stole her."

Wilhelmina retorted, "I didn't technically steal her. I bought her and smuggled her into the country," which made Elsie's eyes get wide. She did not meet Phan until the wedding and, like Nigel, wanted to know more. Nigel and Elsie both stopped chewing.

"Well she was six at the time and fit very easily into my suitcase."

Will chimed in, "My parents had to adopt her to keep Willie from going to jail for human trafficking."

Brother and sister laughed, but Nigel's brows were still raised.

Her face was calm but Vanity's eyes were filled with anger as she explained the whole scenario. A Chinese gang had just bought her from an orphanage and had planned to do not so nice things to a six-year-old girl. Vanity said, "So when I spotted them coming out of the building and one guy pulling up her dress, peeking—I asked to use her for two days."

"In exchange for two hundred American, they gave me the girl. The next day we were leaving Beijing, so I emptied my suitcase and put her inside." She explained that it worked because David had chartered a plane to the next job in Milan.

Vanity chuckled, "David was all like, what do you have in here a couple of bodies?"

"I was never a good liar, so I told him, 'no, only one.'" Vanity's eyes were still intense as she told Nigel and Elsie that David knew something was up because she had kept the suitcase very close to her side. Once they arrived in Milan and the suitcase was opened, that's when David realized she had not been lying.

"David had to use my earnings in Milan to charter another plane back to the U.S. in order to hide Phan."

By now the girl was also laughing, "I was six and didn't know any better. I just knew I was going to America."

She nibbled on an egg, "I'm going to America, I am going to America." Everyone at the counter laughed, "None of us ever considered the pressure from the plane could have popped my eyes out of my head if I had gone below into the cargo hold."

"Well, David did put you and your suitcase on the inside of the plane and when we were airborne, he let you out?" Elsie asked.

Phan yelled again, "I'm going to America!"

Everyone at the table laughed.

Will snacked on a roll of ham, "I have never seen Daddy so mad," they all paused the laughter and Will pointed at Nigel, "Well, that was until you walked into my wedding and started kissing his baby!"

Everyone laughed even harder. Will was still laughing, "I am still trying to get over him socking you in the face." He peered over his glass to look at Nigel's nose and began to laugh even more.

Nigel ignored him, "Phan you grew up with Vanity here in New York?"

"Good Lord, no. Willie was only fifteen when she stole me, and Daddy had just been appointed judge and to avoid an international incident, Mami used her connections in Washington to push through some paperwork." She explained that she was adopted, grew up in Arizona, and had graduated from Arizona State.

Vanity had gotten up to add some grapes to the pile on the table. She threw her arm around her sister, saying, "Phan is a CPA and a grad student at NYU. She has only been in New York a year." Vanity explained that the entire family had attended Arizona State except for Will and her.

Will had attended a private college, then went on to Berkley. "I did my undergrad work in fashion design at the Academy of Art University, then my master's in business at Berkley, along with Will." Nigel sat listening and learning a great deal about his wife. She also explained that Will went on to start his publishing business and she her design business. "David did his grad work at Stanford and invested in both of our businesses to get us up and running."

Nigel asked, "So everything is connected with the family. Khalea, your cousin, is your attorney?"

Will raised his hand and added that she was also his. Nigel looked at Phan, who smiled back at him and said, "I am their personal accountant." Nigel started to laugh. Phan laughed too, "Yes, I keep them both on a tight budget and keep them in the black with their taxes."

Vanity jumped up. "Speaking of which, I did a little freelancing in Vegas." She went into her purse to retrieve the check from the Wynn to hand Phan, who looked at it and asked, "How do you want it dispersed?"

Vanity thought for a second, "Normal bonus for Jessica, add an extra 10% for Clarke for taking care of my husband, and with the rest, start a trust for David's kids, and our soon-to-be arriving nieces and nephews." Phan folded the check and put it in her pocket as she looked at Elsie's belly.

Nigel wanted to know, "So you live here?" He pointed at the floor to see if she lived in the apartment.

Vanity answered, "No, she has her own apartment on this floor, but she has OCD and is always over here messing with my STUFF!"

"She is the one who washed your clothes. She is diabolical, so please don't leave anything lying about," Vanity said at Nigel.

Phan mumbled, "Whatever" and jumped off the seat. "I'm going to be late for class. Is there a car downstairs that can get me across town?" Will made a quick call, and the driver was still with Jessica, so Phan kissed Will, Elsie, and Vanity's cheeks before darting off. She stopped, turned, and came back to kiss Nigel on the cheek as well. "Save me a pork chop, Will, and don't forget to sign the books for tomorrow!"

In a flash she was gone.

WILL LOOKED ABOUT, found the box of books, and began to unpack them on the counter as Elsie helped Vanity clear away the dishes. They did a bit of girl talk and Vanity offered to show her new sister-in-law the apartment and the bedroom she would share with Will while they were in town.

Elsie grinned at her sister-in-law, "All I need to see is your closet!" Arm-in-arm, they headed down the hall to the master bedroom.

Nigel noticed the W.E. Devons books on the countertop and looked at the man on the cover. "Fuck me, is that you one the cover of these books?"

Will continued to unpack the boxes. "Yes, it is me, and no thank you, I don't care how handsome you are."

Nigel picked up Courting Guinevere. "I haven't read this one," he said and started to read the back of the book.

"You are a fan of Devons?"

"Yes..." but he paused, feeling he needed to expound upon why he was reading romance novels. Nigel confided that he had spent six months evaluating one of the factories outside of Dublin. "It was the middle of the winter, and it was a miserable factory and a miserable town, with miserable workers." He confessed to Will that the factory secretary was a huge fan of Devon's work and she gave Nigel a book to read to help keep him calm. "Before I realized it, three months had passed and I had read six of the books, and one I even read twice."

Will watched his brother-in-law's face, waiting for some semblance that he was adding two and two. Nigel turned the book over to see the spine. "Ah, I see Mate, your company publishes these," he took a minute. "Do you think you can get Devons to autograph one for me?"

Will took the book from his hand, removed his favorite pen from his pocket, opened the flap, and wrote, "Oh Brother!" and signed it W.E. Devons. He handed it back to Nigel.

It was almost like watching the stages of self-actualization go across his face. When he finally reached the stage of acceptance, he looked at Will, "Fuck me, I love your work! I am such a big fan! I think this warrants a real kiss there Mate! Your books were a life saver!" Vanity returned to the kitchen to find her husband trying to kiss her brother and her brother fighting him off. She and Elsie stood there wide-eyed and confused.

Will screamed at his sister, "Will you get him off me?"

Vanity didn't know what to say or do. Nigel held up the book, explained about Dublin, and how much he loved Devons work, "Just to think, you are now my brother!"

She and Elsie both exhaled a sigh of relief.

"Will, can I get an autographed copy of all the books? I will buy them if need be."

"As long as you don't try to make out with me again, I will sign anything you want!"

Nigel waved his hand at him and asked, "Why would I want to make out with you when I have her?" His eyes twinkled when he looked at Vanity. She got all doe-eyed.

Will was three steps from gagging and he made the sounds before saying, "Dear Lord, can we get ready for our day of sightseeing?"

Nigel stopped and looked at Will with a face full of uncertainty, "Can I ask what you are going to wear?"

Will looked at his sister, "I am going to wear what I have on." He was dressed in Khakis and a long-sleeved polo shirt.

Nigel looked at Vanity as well. "Can I wear what he is wearing?" Will wasn't privy to the private joke but Vanity laughed hard as she pulled her husband down the hallway to get changed for their outing. "Nigel, you can pick you own clothing and dress yourself you know," she said with a smile.

{17] Waking the giant...

It had been a very full day with Will, Elsie and sightseeing around New York City. Elsie was excited about visiting the Metropolitan Museum of Art, and she tried to coax Nigel and Vanity into coming along. Nigel was quick to refuse, telling her, "I grew up in a museum. I have no desire to visit one for amusement."

After dinner, full on pork chops and Elsie's macaroni and cheese, sleep was calling, but instead the group opted for some family time. Phan favored the group with a few piano selections, and Nigel took the opportunity to dance with Elsie since he had not been able to at the wedding. The last selection of the evening, Vanity played a version of "Peel Me A Grape," which began a vibrant discussion among the four on the potentiality of grape peeling.

It was difficult to hide his shock after dinner when Vanity invited him into the kitchen to help with the cleanup. "Since they cooked, we do the cleanup, and vice versa when we visit them." He only nodded and waited for her instructions on what he needed to rinse, dry, and put away. She noticed him smiling as he carefully cared for each dish.

"In all of my life," he told her, "this is the first time I have ever done the dishes."

Her hands in rubberized gloves, she thumbed water at him, "Stick with me, Your Grace, and I am going to introduce you to all sorts of new stuff."

Her tone was playful but her eyes were not.

He understood her taunt and chimed in, "I was thinking the same thing, Darling."

Tonight, would be the first night they were truly alone in their bed. He said nothing more, but continued to work and watched with interest as she sprayed and wiped down the counters, measured the leftovers and put them into containers in the fridge, and wiped down the stove. The whole process, including the dish washing, took a half hour.

Later, in bed, Nigel kissed her lips lightly, held her hand as he moved a tad closer to her, and was off to sleep. Vanity's mind was racing and the smell of Nigel was igniting her senses. At the sound of his even breathing, she eased away from him to have a little late-night yoga workout to settle herself. This was a first for her. Although she had worked with and around some of the best-looking best-looking men in the world, she never found herself stimulated by them, let alone needing to settle herself so she could sleep through the night. But her husband had her rethinking many of her opinions on men and sex. Mostly, she was rethinking her views on sex. Especially, sex with him.

AT SIX AM, HER BODY was wide awake and craving his touch. This was a first for her, and she didn't know how to handle it. He was her husband. She should be able to talk to him about her needs. But finding the right way to ask was the main problem, second only to him still sleeping. *I don't even know what my needs are; how the bleep do I ask for him to help me?* The first thing she needed was to get comfortable with a very virile man in her life and in her bed.

The first rays of morning light were starting to stream through the small windows above the bed and she inched the covers down his chest so she could see his body. Her hand meandered under the covers. Tentative fingers slid under his tee to feel the wispy hairs on his abdomen. Curiosity urged her on to feel the hairs on his chest. In the past two days, he had given her two eyefuls; one of him naked and the other in his early morning state. Her traitorous body twitched, her mind said touch him, and her breasts felt as if they were swelling. She needed to feel more of him.

Her hand moved lower as she pushed aside his boxers to take hold of the bulbs which held their future children. *These two little things here are the bringers of life.* She gently rolled them in her hands. *His berries.* She felt the larger part of him move against her hand. *Oho, the twig wants to play too!* Disregarding his reaction, she persisted with the gentle massage, enjoying the texture of the skin in comparison to other parts of his body. Using her hands to smooth down the hairs on his thighs, she slowly came back and noticed that now another part of him was fully awake. It almost called to her as it sat up, erect and craving her attention.

Well, I don't want the poor fella to feel unloved, so she took it in her hand.

It was warm in her hands. "Hello there Guv'nah!" She said to Nigel's attached buddy using a Cockney British accent.

A tightening of her grip elicited movement from Nigel's legs. Vanity turned to her side, resting her head on Nigel's chest as she tightened her grip again while using her other hand to cup the life givers. His legs moved again. This position is all wrong. She shifted the way she was sitting next to him by coming to her knees and kneeling beside him in the bed.

Her hand was firmly wrapped around him as she employed a gentle downward stroking action which made his toes splay open and then curl. His body seemed to like what she was doing, so she did it again, this time with a firmer grip. She heard Nigel grunt. She slowly lifted her head to look at this face in the dimly lit room, and his eyes were still closed. Just a little more and she would leave him to his sleep, but she had to admit that it was an impressive tool. She needed more friction. She quickly unhanded him, spit in her hand, and stroked him some more. Now, he was moving his legs and his hips.

The groan that came from his throat, surprisingly, turned her on, so much so that she forgot she had told herself that she would stop her act. Especially since he was responding fully to what she was doing and she loved it. She shifted her weight again on the bed and gave him her full attention: grip, stroke, leg movement.

Okay, he likes that.

Pressure, rub faster, stroke, slow down, and wait. No movement of the legs. Noted. He doesn't like that as much, back to the original technique.

She now had a firm grip with her left hand. She stroked hard, cupped the life givers with her right, and gave them a gentle massage, and he moaned and thrust his hips.

He really likes that.

She gave him more. He was moving with her strokes and his breathing was becoming labored. Vanity thought she had better stop before she woke him. When she looked at his face, he was wide awake and looking at her. Oh Silk! Her eyes grew wide at being caught violating him in his sleep.

His hands moved to his sides as he gripped the sheets, sunk his teeth into his bottom lip, and began to slowly move in her hand. Nigel's eyes never left hers as he encouraged her to finish him off. She cupped and massaged the life givers, his brow furrowed, and his heavy breathing increased. She gripped him hard, looking into his eyes, and stroked downward. He raised up in the bed to his elbows.

She stroked him harder.

Nigel threw back his head and gave into the pleasure his wife was gifting him. It felt heavenly to him and he could not remember the last time he had, "Ohhhh," was all that came out as he continued to move into her hand, emptying out a year's worth of long hours, late nights, and loneliness. The longer she held and stroked him, the more he seemed to produce. When he finally stopped spewing forth his pent-up desires, he looked at his wife whose eyes were wide in disbelief. She was also frowning. Vanity Devons had a physical facial reaction.

Her hand was held up and was completely covered in his DNA. She tried to shake it off like it was a sticky booger that would not go away. "What are you, Spiderman?" she asked.

Nigel quickly removed his tee shirt and started to wipe her hands like a small child after they had eaten their first ice cream cone as he told her, "It's been a bit, okay Love?"

Vanity would not let it go. "A bit?" she asked him. "Is that a British unit of time measurement for two-and-a-half years? Do you produce that much every time? Holy Silk Sheeting! Are you planning to impregnate me or start an Army of minions?"

She was laughing but he was not amused. He continued to use the shirt to clean himself up and removed the stained clothing, but now he was completely nude in the bed. She could not help but appreciate the beauty of his body. Vanity was about to push the envelope and tell him she would have to wear protective gear if they did that again, but she noticed a different look in his eyes.

"I do like to reciprocate, my Dear," he said and he reached for her. She wasn't fast enough to get off the bed and he had her pinned under his thigh. "Time to dust the cobwebs off you as well, Spidergirl."

Nigel slowly lifted her pajama top to expose her breasts. The cool bedroom air hardened the buds and he lowered his head to take one in his mouth. Her struggling stopped and she went limp as he grazed his teeth across the sensitive skin. He gathered her in his arms, rolling to his back, then to his left side, depositing her gently on the bed. Slowly, she helped raise the top over her head until both breasts were exposed, and he licked his palm. She watched as his right hand lowered over her left breast and made circular motions over the nipple while his mouth brought pleasure to the right. Her legs began to move.

Is this what my body was telling me it needed?

He cupped the right breast and massaged it and gently squeezed the teat between his thumb and forefinger. A rush of feeling shot to her nether region and her legs clenched together. He moved over her body and took the left nipple in his mouth whilst his right hand made its way down her body. She wore Capri-style pajama pants and he needed her out of them. "Off," he spoke softly, "can we take these off?" She followed his instructions and quickly removed the pants. For some reason, she left the underpants on and waited for his instructions.

Gentle fingers rubbed the cotton fabric of her panties and then slipped in between her thighs to find their prize. The touch of his hand there brought her hands up into his hair, pulling his face closer to her breast and his fingers, awakened something inside of her, setting her body afire. He rubbed gently and she moved against his hand. Nigel stopped the movement to look at her face. She looked angered that he had ceased giving her pleasure, but as he watched her face, his hand moved to the top of the waistband of her panties. She said nothing. His four fingers slid inside the material to feel a Brazilian wax job with a landing strip. Vanity continued to watch his face as his index finger made contact with her... "Oh my," she breathed heavily, and he applied pressure. "Goodness!" was all she could say as one finger went far enough down to collect moisture, but not far enough to be invasive. Nigel set to work.

Within minutes, Vanity was deep into her pleasure, and when Nigel brought his mouth back to her breast, she let go. Since there was company in the house, he muffled her mouth with his own and she passionately responded while she moved against his hand. This one was a real wildcat and Nigel was loving every minute of it, but at this rate, she would be pregnant by the end of the day. His body was ready again, and he wanted to make a first attempt at making love to her, but was interrupted by a knock at the door. He quickly grabbed the bed covers and covered their bodies.

Through a dry and raspy throat, she called out, "Yeah?"

Will opened the door and popped his head inside, "Hey Willie," he started to say, but noticed the large wedding photo of the two of them over the bed. That was fast. He could not help but notice how happy and beautiful his sister looked in the photo, but his eyes were drawn back to the movement in the bed. "Sorry, Willie, Elsie and I were wondering if you wanted to join us this morning for yoga."

She giggled, "Well, I kind of worked out a little already this morning." The thought of what she was implying made Will draw up a bit. His sister didn't giggle! Willie wasn't a giggling sort of woman.

Nigel responded before Will could even react, as he came out from under the covers, "What do you mean, kind of?"

The Duke had sat up in the bed and his chest was bare, and hair was completely disheveled. Will thought him to be a hairy fella but noticed his sister was without a top. Nigel gave him a direct stare, "Unless you want to hear my wife find religion this morning, I suggest you close and lock that door, Mate." Nigel pulled the covers over their heads while telling Vanity, "I'll give you a workout, Spidergirl!" Vanity giggled again like a school girl.

"Oh Nigel..."

Will hurriedly closed the door. He stood on the outside of the entrance looking sickened. There is a man in my sister's bed! They are doing stuff to each other! Will felt the bile rise in his throat. He was hit with a rush of emotion and thought out loud, "Oh dear God, no."

Elsie came out of their room and stood in front of him. "Will, did you ask her to join us?"

He shook his head yes as his hand covered his mouth and he looked at his wife, who was not paying much attention, "Well, Will, is she coming?" Elsie asked.

Will grabbed his stomach and began to walk quickly towards the kitchen. Passing his wife, he could hear his sister's voice as she began her morning prayers, yelling, "Oh bless me... this has to be a sin. Dear God, yes... Nigel, yes!"

Will grabbed Elsie by the hand and muttered, "Sounds like it," as they made their way towards the kitchen and Will started to cook breakfast.

Elsie noticed the tinge of discoloration around his mouth and asked, "Will, can you feel what she is feeling?" Elsie had heard that twins could sometimes do that.

He continued to whip the eggs to make omelets. "When we are in prox-imity, yes, and intense emotions we can feel, no matter how far apart we are." Will stopped and stared into space. He clutched at his stomach and looked at his wife with an almost sick hue about him.

Elsie had to know. "Did you feel what she just felt?"

Will looked sick, "I feel an intense emotion and butterflies in my stomach."

They both remained quiet. Elsie continued to push, "Is this the first time you have felt this?"

Will poured the first omelet mix into the pan. "Actually, it is." He wasn't sure if it was because he was here in the apartment with her because he knew it was not her first time with a man.

Elsie was smiling at him, "Well you know what this means right?"

Will handed her a completed omelet and made one for him. "Yes," he mut-tered as he completed his breakfast and joined her at the table, "it means it's time for us to leave."

Vanity Devons was in good hands.

{18} Time to go to work...

After a quick breakfast and a farewell to her brother- and sister-in-law, Vanity knew she had to get back to work. Will had been kind and made her and Nigel omelets, but she passed on the flipped over eggs and she packed them a lunch and headed downstairs to work. Nigel set up in the corner of her office and checked in with his staff. He made calls, checked on orders, and verified shipments of the fabric to her New York office as well as the fabric that would ship to the manufacturing division in California.

At 11 am, he sat in on her meeting with Jessica and Clarke as they went over in detail the Milan show. He was surprised at how much responsibility they both held and even more so with the vast amount of responsibility that was held by Clarke. He wasn't just the person who did her hair and make-up, Clarke was the Creative Director for all of Vanity Devon's fashion shows.

She gave them both marching directions and explained that she needed to see the final designs before she left for London next week and a dry run through the following Thursday when they met her at Nigel's country estate in the Cotswold District. Nigel added, "It is outside of Gloucester."

He noticed Jessica making notes, and she looked at him, "Your Grace, is there anywhere to land a plane?" Nigel shook his head no, looking at her with some concern.

Nigel heard a small bell chime and the meeting was ended. It was now time for lunch and he was starving. Vanity removed from the fridge two lunch containers. To Nigel, she handed a chicken salad sandwich with wedges of cheddar and double Gloucester, along with grapes and fresh berries. Jessica had already put on the kettle and he was surprised when his wife's employees joined them at the table in the break room. Jessica poured his water for his tea and brought over a box of English teas for him to choose from.

During the meal, there was no talk of work. They talked of plans for vacation and Clarke turned the conversation to Nigel, "Your Grace, what is your most favorite thing to do in your down time?"

Nigel sat his teacup down and said, "I love to shoot." He explained that he truly enjoyed spending as much time as he could at his home in Cotswold where he often would hunt quail or just shoot clays, "I think it is what you would call Skeet shooting." Jessica asked a few questions, Vanity asked one, and then the conversation moved on.

Nigel listened to them talk then he asked Jessica, "If money were no object, Jessica, what would you love to do?"

Clarke piped in before she had a chance to answer, "I would be in Abu Dhabi!" Nigel only smiled at Clarke but kept his eyes trained on Jessica. She finally answered him, "I would do a month-long travel blog about eating my way through South America."

"Just a month?"

Jessica finished her meal and took her plates to the sink. "Maybe two, then back to work," she responded.

Vanity knew Nigel well enough to understand that any question he asked was for good reason, but for now, she would make no inquiries about his intentions. He was a surprising man, and he continued to earn more of her trust when he took her plate from the table, made dishwater, and washed their dishes. He even dried them and put them back in the lunch bags. Clarke and Jessica watched in amazement. He even washed his tea cup and left it on a napkin to drain. Nigel turned to find everyone staring at him.

"Well, I will need it again for afternoon tea," he told them.

The afternoon progressed nicely and Nigel was able to get a great deal completed while his wife met with two department store merchandisers. Each attempt they made to strong arm her into placing her products in their stores she refuted with professionalism and grace. He heard the chime again as his wife took a break for an afternoon snack. She dismissed her business guests, showing them to the door, and moved her way back to the kitchen and made tea for him with lemon cakes and fresh strawberries. "Are you eating on a schedule Wilhelmina?"

"Yes, I must balance out my glycemic index," she explained that she had never, and would never, diet, be a fad eater, or torture her body. "I eat small meals all day which boosts my metabolism, so I can enjoy what I want." She nibbled on a strawberry and snacked on a piece of cheddar, adding, "Since I am never hungry, I don't have any cravings or am prone to eat things I shouldn't."

She smiled at him, "I have been the same weight since I was 15 years old and the same size." Nigel was happy to know she did not have any eating disorders and that meal time was not going to be a total pain in the ass with him forced to graze on leafy greens of foliage and a sliver of meat. Vanity made a point of telling him, "I eat just about everything, including carbs, but I don't eat beef." He asked no questions, and she took care of clean up.

They worked until about 5:45 and she started to close up shop. "Are you done for the day?" he wanted to know.

Vanity explained they only worked from ten until six pm unless there was a show coming up or a heavy production schedule. "When we return from Milan, we go into production to fill orders, and then we begin the winter catalogs." She explained that her catalogs were only filled with items that were not sold at shows.

At six fifteen, Nigel was starving and asked her about food, "Are we going to order something, or should we call a car to take us to dinner?" She waved her finger for him to follow her in the kitchen.

"Wash your hands and come join me." She removed four chicken breasts from the fridge that had marinated all day. "Nigel, I very rarely, if ever, eat out."

"You are cooking?" he asked incredulously as she butterflied and pounded the chicken breasts.

"I cook all my meals, unless of course, one of my brothers is here, then I let him cook." He watched her place the grill over the eyes of the stove. Vanity washed the asparagus, cleaned it, and threw it in the steamer. Brown rice with chicken stock was added to the rice cooker, and he watched in amazement as she prepped, prepared, and plated their dinner. With patience and care, Vanity showed him how to wash the Romaine and tomatoes as he prepared the salads. Next, she demonstrated how to make her favorite dressing of olive oil, white wine vinegar, lemon juice and fresh herbs. There was also a nice choice of wines for dinner.

"Halley bought David a vineyard as a wedding present. He is training to be a Sommelier, and he has a great palate. Most of these wines are his selections. A few are mine."

As they dined, he told her of his country home and she was excited to meet the people who lived in the town. Nigel helped with the dishes and looked about, wondering what they would do next since they were alone. What was on his mind was not what was on hers.

"We have two choices," she laughed, "we can choose a movie or have live music."

His interest was piqued, "I will go with the live music." After a quick refill of his wine glass and hers as well, she took a seat at the piano. Hazel eyes looked towards the ceiling as she tapped into her musical repertoire. Vanity's face lit up with a smile. Adept hands glided across the keys as she began a jazz standard of "A Lazy Afternoon." Nigel nearly dropped his glass when a clear soprano voice started singing along as she as she played with the music.

Next, Vanity played a classical piece of Mozart, and then went back to an Ella Fitzgerald's version of "Misty." Nigel found himself filled with emotion as she finished her last song. His beautiful and extremely talented wife was a gift to him from Heaven. It would never matter what it was she wanted, he would move the mountains to make her happy.

When he mentioned he didn't know she played, "I was classically trained from the age of five until I was about eleven, but I heard this jazz song coming from my Dad's home office and was hooked!" She was still lit up like a Christmas tree as she spoke, "Mamí was furious, but I spent the rest of my years in between modeling gigs learning to play nothing but jazz. It is my thing. An art class or design class, jazz immersion camps, and David always made sure my downtime had things that I loved to do." She rose and took a sip from her glass, "I guess jazz just speaks to me." Nigel understood because her music spoke to him.

Vanity explained, "I guess out of all of my parent's children, I was the artsy fartsy one, while David had a gift for numbers and language, and Will had a gift for words and perfect pitch. You should hear him sing... his singing voice is amazing."

She sat beside him in a comfortable lounger, "If I had not modeled, I would have been an actress or a jazz pianist." He knew she had been in several large Hollywood productions and was a pretty decent actress. They would talk about that later, but right now, the only thing on his mind was being close to her, connecting with her on a deeper level.

Nigel Strathmore was in love. Head over heels, heart beating fast, sweaty palms, goo-goo gaga head over heels in love. He gently removed the wine goblet from her hand and took it to the kitchen. He returned to put on a song he saw earlier in the CD player, pulling her into his arms and dancing while holding her close. It was self-understood that he was lost and completely under her spell. He wanted nothing more than to feel her hands on him again and he danced her all the way to the bedroom. There were many things he wanted to show and teach her, but there would be time.

Nigel considered the way she chose to start their morning, even if it had been a curious accident. This evening, it would be done with purpose with a simultaneous ending. There were so many ways to teach Vanity the ways of pleasure, even if he had to hand it to her on a silver platter.

{19} Understanding the standard...

Vanity didn't seem to be surprised when she walked into the kitchen and found her brother David putting on coffee. She placed a light kiss on his cheek as she noticed the book on the counter top, The Light Between Two Oceans by M.L. Steadman. "Good morning my vain one, did you finish reading this novel?"

"I did, but I don't agree with the note you left me about Isabel and her choices on the child," Vanity told him which spurred an early morning debate between the two. "Speaking of a child, you are away from yours so soon after their births. I know Halley isn't happy about that."

David only grinned, "I am not too happy about it either. They are beautiful babies and I can't wait to get back, but I had some things to still square up at corporate headquarters. I am being given some freelance work. I had to come in person."

Nigel could hear the voices from the kitchen as well as the smell of bacon frying. Clad in a loose tee and lounge pants, he made his way to the kitchen. Today was day nine of his stay in America and what he wanted to witness above all else was now taking place. He needed to see his wife's interaction with her brother David.

Initially upon meeting her, he believed that the man she held in highest regard was her father, who set the standard of how she viewed men. However, after meeting the dad, it was obvious that she loved her parents, but wasn't necessarily close with them because of so much time on the road. Maybe her connection is with her twin? After spending a day or so with her Wilfred, it was apparent they shared a close bond, but this brother was not the standard, either.

A twinge of jealously rose up in Nigel as he watched her converse with her big brother. Her face completely radiated light as they bantered back and forth over a book he had never heard of. A loose tendril of her hair fell across her face and David carefully pushed it behind her ear as he continued to bombard her with reasons why Tom should have made a better decision.

Who the bloody hell is Tom?

David answered him, "Tom is the main character in the story, Your Grace. Good morning." Nigel didn't realize he had spoken the question aloud.

Vanity wasted no time, still arguing with David and greeting her husband with a kiss and a cup of tea as David placed bacon and eggs in front of him. By the sounds of the conversation, his wife was winning the argument, but David had an ace up his sleeve.

"Your Grace...," he started, but Nigel stopped him.

"We are brothers now. Please use my given name," he said.

"As you wish. Nigel, here is the argument. As husbands, it is our duty to make our wives happy, but where do you draw the line? Especially when you know your decision is the impacting result of someone else's happiness?"

Nigel frowned, "I can't answer that question David because I do not have all the facts or all the variables to make an informed decision."

"EXACTLY!" David said, but Vanity wasn't done. She placed her hand inside of Nigel's.

"Husband," she said, staring deep into his eyes.

"Yes, my wife?" He found himself grinning at her.

"If the only thing I ever wanted was a ruby ring and on the way home from work, you witnessed a bank robbery, and the robber is shot and dies at your feet with the bag full of money. No one is there but you. You don't take it all, just enough to buy me that ruby ring. Would you confess to your thievery, knowing you are giving me the one thing I truly want?"

He ran his fingers across his morning stubble, "I probably would not because as your husband, my main desire is to keep you happy and content. It was a gift that just showed up at my feet, so I probably would take full advantage of the circumstance."

"EXACTLY" Vanity yelled!

David handed the book to Nigel, retorting, "Exactly my ass Mina! It was a child, not a stone that was dug out of the earth. It was a human child who belonged to someone else who is mourning the loss of said child and then there is Isabel with this woman's baby!"

Nigel chimed in, "Wait, darling, David as a point. That is an entirely different kettle of fish."

For the second time in nine days, Vanity Devons made a face at him, "And tonight you are sleeping on the couch, Your Grace!"

That did it for Nigel. He jumped up and ran to the door, "David, you are dead wrong and you may leave these premises right away!"

It was the start of a very good day. Laughter, good food, and hearty conversation began a new day as well as a newfound appreciation for his wife. He liked the way her mind worked.

BECAUSE OF THE NUMBER of meetings that Vanity had that day, Nigel opted to remain in the apartment, grateful for the opportunity to spend time in the company of David. There were things on his mind and he knew why her brother was here.

"Might I have a word with you today, David?"

"Of course, Your...," David stopped himself, "Nigel."

"I was wondering if you wouldn't mind taking me out today for the midday meal? I am feeling a bit light-headed and am in need of a hunk of red meat, some friend potatoes, and a pint."

"Not a problem. I would be honored to do so," David said as he collected his things.

"It will be my treat of course. I heard about this place." Nigel grabbed the magazine he had been saving and pointed at the ad for Delmonico's. "I would like to go here. And I want the Lobster Newberg, a steak, and the baked Alaska."

"Well, we'd better leave now," David said but Nigel didn't move. He was rooted to the floor.

"Is everything okay Nigel?"

He was almost embarrassed to ask, but the last few days had made him a bit sensitive, "Is what I am wearing fitting?"

David didn't understand the question. Nigel Strathmore had better taste in clothing than he did and was always impeccably tailored. He thought about his sister and her desire to be picture perfect and he began to laugh. In black lightweight woolen slacks, loafers, and a cardigan over a cream-colored shirt, the Duke looked like he just stepped out of GQ Magazine.

"You look sharp, Your Grace. Let me take you out to see New York my way," David told him as he sent his sister a message that he was taking the Duke to lunch. A lunch that began a conversation David had been waiting to have with his Lordship for nearly a year.

THE RESTAURANT LOOKED exactly as it did in the picture, and Nigel was excited when his medium rare steak arrived. "Excuse me Madam, I would like a pint, please."

The waitress, a pleasant looking blonde, "Ooh you're British. You remind me of a young Pierce Brosnan."

Nigel was polite, "I get that a lot."

It was a blowoff and the waitress got it, but came back to the table to hit on David who was far less nice. When she flirted with them both, David informed her nicely that they were married.

"To each other? Such a shame," the waitress said as she clucked her tongue.

David pulled out a few bills from his wallet, "After you take care of our check, you can keep it all, if you promise not to come back to this table."

In a huff and indignant, she took the money and sauntered away. An older waitress later returned to the table to fill their drink glasses and the meal progressed pleasantly when David finally looked up and said, "Spit it out, Nigel."

"Was I that obvious Mate?"

"Yes. What do you want to know?"

It took a few breaths but he finally was able to put it into words, "How do I do this?"

"Do what Nigel?

He exhaled loudly, "It is obvious that her standard for men in her life is based on her relationship with you. I am just not sure how I..." His words were low. Nigel appeared uncertain of what to say next, so David spoke.

"Until I quit my job a few months back, I was in Asia at least six times per year. I could get silk wholesale a hell of a lot cheaper than I am getting it from you." David said as he took a swig of beer that had turned warm. "You are perfect for my sister, which is why I chose you."

Nigel's mouth was wide, then he closed it. "How do I make this work David? I have to be honest, as far as I planned was getting on the plane, marrying her, and getting home without needing to wear a little white coat where I hug myself all day. I would be happy just to get home and not be a total nutter after flying."

What could David tell his brother-in-law that would make sense and pull all the pieces together? He knew the perfect analogous segue.

He spoke slowly. "Although I am her brother and served as her manager and later business partner, every week I took my sister on a date. We would dress up and go out, and each week I would give Mina a new book to read with a moral dilemma. These would be our points of discussion for the evening. We had deep conversations on how the decisions made by supporting characters would impact the lives of others. There was never any talk about work, what was next on her calendar, or her personal career goals. It was my time with my little sister."

Nigel was bobbing his head, "Like I saw this morning?"

"Yes, pretty much. She is truly a special woman with more talent than she knows what to do with..."

"I cannot believe I am going to ask you this but, how can I be a good husband to her?"

"Create a world in your world that encompasses hers. She can work from anywhere, but she is a creature of habit. Make your world match the one she lives in and she will be happy. But most of all, never objectify her or treat like she is stupid."

"I can do that," Nigel said feeling much better about moving forward.

"I have one question for you, Nigel," David said as he sliced into his steak. "Do you enjoy talking to her?"

The grin that covered Nigel's face was almost priceless, "I fell in love after our second conversation."

That was more than enough for David.

THE NEXT DAY SPED BY in a blur and Finley called Friday morning, informing the Duke that he was at the airport, fueled and ready to go. Nigel didn't know if he was more concerned about leaving his wife or getting on that bloody plane for nearly ten hours. "Nigel, my handsome husband," Vanity said, and he stopped and turned to face her, "I am truly going to miss seeing that sexy naked bum every morning."

As she moved closer, he started to laugh and replied, "In less than a week, I will be in your arms again." She kissed him while subtly reminding him of all the things that had to be done to prep for her arrival. "I am excited to meet your parents, brother, sister, and friends and see your home in Gloucester and the London townhouse."

Nigel's mind started to race. "You are right there is a lot to do." He grabbed his watch, and Clarke had already taken his things down to the car. He shook Clarke's hand, hugged Jessica and Phan, and kissed his wife. "See you in a week, Darling." And her husband was gone.

Nigel called her that night to let her know he had made it home safely, and during their week apart, he called her every morning after her yoga workout. Vanity called him every evening right before dinner. She missed her husband and by Thursday night, she was ready to see her man. Chuck was sitting on the Tarmac at Meadowlands fueled and ready to depart when she arrived. Vanity was in such a hurry that she would have forgotten her rolling cooler had it not been for Jessica reminding her. She climbed inside to find a passenger on her plane who said, "I am sorry Willie, but I had to get away."

{20] My new intern...

Vanity smiled at her nephew Gianni and took a close look at the expression on his face and in his eyes and understood that things at his house had changed, and maybe he felt a little out of place.

"G-Pop said this would be the first time you would be doing the Milan show without one of your brothers, and that he was concerned," he told Vanity, and she smiled because that was just like her dad subtly convinced the men in their family that she was a damsel in distress.

Gianni said, "So I told him, I was free over the holidays and also the summer after I graduate and I hadn't traveled much, and I could be your escort."

"Gianni, you said that you had to get away. Is everything okay at home?" Although she knew the answer, she would give him a chance to say to someone what was bothering his young mind.

"Naww," he said as he secured her cooler of food stores. He also helped Chuck secure the doors and did the crosscheck for takeoff. Vanity noticed how much he knew about prepping for flight, thought about his work on the ranch, and was struck with a brilliant idea. She sat and secured herself in the seat after a nod to Chuck that they were ready.

"It's just," he took a seat across from her, "you know with the babies coming, all the talk around the house is about childproofing, the nursery. I just needed to stretch a bit."

Chuck had already received his clearance for takeoff, and they were taxing and in the air in less than five minutes.

"Gianni," she told him, "those babies will never replace your Dad's love for you."

Gianni's eyes were kind of misting, "Yeah, but you know, they are his blood – me, G-Pop handed me to him to take care of." He turned his head to hide his tears.

"Gianni, you saved my brother's life," she told him, unbuckling her seatbelt, gently easing into the seat next to him, and sliding her arms around his shoulder. "Before you came into his life, he was a mess. You helped him heal. Taking care of you saved him from becoming a crazy person." She pulled him close and kissed him on the head, "You are our blood, you are our family, and you," she handed him her handkerchief, "are a Devonshire!"

She saw a smile as he wiped away his tears. "Now, traveling with me, means you work. Everyone on my team has a job. Your first job is my personal security. It is imperative that I never go anywhere alone and you never, ever, leave me completely alone, unless I specifically request it."

He nodded. She touched the overhead button, "Chuck are we okay for electronics?"

"As my new paid intern, there is a great deal of prep work that has to happen before the show. I am going to put you in charge of these items." She handed him her tablet and removed a second one from her bag. The remainder of the flight, she explained her business, what they would do on this trip, and the plans for the Milan show.

Gianni was a smart kid. He took in the information with confidence and ease, even when she said that he might have to double as one of the models if she needed an extra man. He took it all in stride.

"So, Willie," he asked sheepishly, "you actually married that 007 dude?"

THE THREE ARRIVED IN London on time and Vanity was surprised to see Finley there to greet them. Nigel's pilot had given Chuck specific landing instructions for a private airfield that was only used by the Royal family. Finley would bring Chuck to the house later after they had spent some time in London. She knew Chuck. He would want to sleep first.

Gianni began to jump up and down when he saw the Bentley waiting to escort them into London. Vanity gave him a disapproving look as they climbed inside. "Emotions are always in check, Gianni. This is a very critical week and we want to make a good impression. Listen closely to everything that is being said and pick up on the subtle cues," she told him as the driver closed the door.

"The dude said it was the royal air field. Is your husband royalty? My dad said 007 had a dukedom or a douche or something; what does that mean Willie?"

"It is called a duchy. He is a Duke and it means that the Queen is Nigel's Great Aunt," she said hoping that his teen brain would calculate the rest. It must have pacified him because he was quiet as they drove through the back fields behind Buckingham Palace, through the gates and into London.

Once they arrived at the townhouse, Vanity's stomach was full of butterflies worrying that her husband might not have missed her as much as she missed him. She would play it cool and she even dressed conservatively with brown slacks, a soft peach two-piece cardigan set, and graduated pearls. Her hair was in a chignon and her bag was a modest size. Gianni helped with her cooler, and she carried her business satchel with the extra tablet.

Since they were expected, there was no need to ring the doorbell as they were greeted at the door by a butler who welcomed them both. As they entered the parlor, she was impressed with the space of the inside, and the Strathmore coat of arms seemed to adorn every fixture in the home, including the floor tiles.

"Milady, I am Giles, your Lordship's personal butler." Gianni's eyebrows went up in surprise. "If you would follow me," he said with regal bearing, his back straight as a rod, he led them to an office where Nigel sat behind a desk in a meeting with two gentlemen, appearing totally bored and distracted until Giles announced her arrival. Nigel looked up at her and the smile on his face totally made her melt.

"Gentlemen, I would like to present to you Lady Wilhelmina," Nigel proclaimed.

Both men turned and she heard an audible gasp from the more handsome of the two. Nigel walked around the desk and Vanity noticed he was impeccably dressed in deep green trousers with matching deep green loafers, a grey waist coat, and a speckled tie that brought it all together. He wore a fitted jacket to match the pants and he looked like a glass of cool lemonade on a hot Arizona day. Her body started feeling tingly.

The gentlemen both bowed over her hand as she was introduced to Sir Roddy Piker and Sir Thomas Mulroy, two of Nigel's best friends from Oxford. Sir Roddy was the first to ask, "Nigel, old chap, who is the delightful creature?"

Nigel took her into his arms, "Lady Wilhelmina is my wife." His friends were in shock as he briefly kissed Vanity, only to notice Gianni standing there.

"Well, hello there, nephew," he said as he shook the boy's hand and welcomed him to London. "Giles, will take your things to your room."

Gianni appeared to be a bit reluctant and seemed uncertain of what he should do next. His aunt's instructions were to never leave her alone. He was certain if leaving her with Nigel and two strange men counted as alone?

Nigel helped break the ice. "Gianni, last week in New York, your father cooked the most amazing pork chops."

Sir Roddy and Sir Thomas both asked at the same time, "You were in New York?"

Nigel turned back to them both, "Yes, I flew first to..." he paused and looked at his wife.

"Arizona," she added.

"Ah, yes," Nigel said. "And then on to Vegas and back to New York." His friends stood gape-jawed.

"Now Gianni, do you know how to make those chops your Dad cooks?"

Gianni had relaxed a bit and answered slowly, "I can, but Lady Wilhelmina makes lamb chops that put those to shame."

Vanity was pleased that he had taken the cues. He slowed down as he used the proper name in front of Nigel's friends and referred to her as Lady Wilhelmina, versus Willie.

Sir Thomas piped in, "You can cook, Lady Wilhelmina, and are a delight to the eye as well?"

It was Sir Roddy who stole the show. He said, with a great amount of pride, "I do say, you are quite lovely M'Lady, however, you cannot hold a torch to my beauty Vanity Devons."

Gianni stared with a what the what what? look on his face that nearly made Nigel burst out laughing, but he was curious how his wife was going to handle this one.

"Are you dating Vanity Devons?" she asked with a straight face.

The smug look on Sir Roddy's face was priceless, "No, not yet, but soon. The American will be my wife before you know it."

Vanity was still puzzled, especially considering she had no recollection of ever meeting the man, "Ah, so she has no idea of your undying love for her? You have spent time with this Devons?"

He lowered his head, inhaling softly as if to recount a wonderful memory. "I met her briefly in Milan last year. I even sent her flowers hued of passion pink to match the bloom on her cheeks. I look forward to seeing her again at her show next week."

There were ten bouquets sent backstage but only one of pink roses, Vanity recalled. Nigel and Gianni watched her face as she moved closer to Sir Roddy to make her next words intimate, but not inappropriate. "Next time, bring daisies," she whispered, and the Duke watched his friend's head pop up to stare his wife in the face. "Daisies are my favorite. I do believe I sent you a thank you for the pink roses. They were lovely."

Sir Roddy started to sputter as Giles moved behind him and Sir Thomas to usher them out the door. Once they left, Gianni, Nigel, and Vanity burst into laughter. Nigel turned to Gianni, "So, Gianni, have you ever driven a Ferrari?"

Gianni thought that if cooking some pork chops was all it took to drive a beautiful car like that, then it was a deal. He was now glad he made the choice to come along with his Aunt.

{21] Introducing M'lady...

T he small staff was lined up in the dining room to meet the new lady of the house. Giles, Nigel's butler, often traveled with him and rarely left his side except for the trip to the US. In Vanity's opinion, Giles was rather young to be a butler, appearing to be in his early forties. When asked, he stated with pride, "My family has served the Strathmore's all our lives, M 'Lady, and it is my honor to continue the tradition."

The housekeeper was also Nigel's personal caregiver and took care of the Cotswold estate, his quarters in Strathmore Keep, and the townhouse. There was a separate staff for the Villa in Milan. Where ever his Lordship resided, she was there. Her name was Maddie.

The cook, named Biddie, had a warm face and very bad teeth, but was delighted to meet them both. She was even more surprised when Vanity asked, "Ms. Biddie, I am on a restricted diet, would it be okay if I helped you prepare my meals?" Biddie's eyebrows shot up, and she looked to Nigel for guidance, but Vanity stepped into her line of sight between her husband and the servant, "If it is too much trouble, I can prepare my own."

"No M'Lady, we will have no such thing. You show Biddie how to make ye vittles, and I will take care of the cooking for ye," the cook sputtered over her words. It was uncertain if she had a Cockney accent, with a Gaelic undertone, or if the bad teeth just made her tongue tied.

Last was a young woman who seemed very timid but had kind eyes. Nigel introduced her as Babette and said, "She will take care of your personal needs, your laundry, hair care, make-up, and anything else you should require." Vanity was touched that he had hired someone for her personally, but the young lady looked terrified.

Vanity extended her hand, "Pleasure to have you at my side." She pulled the pins from her hair and let the mass fall. "I was so afraid that his Lordship would have to help me manage this nightmare I call hair." Babette swore in French and placed her hands over her mouth at her unprofessional response and Vanity lapsed into her caretaker's language and explained her hair care routine.

Nigel's eyes were wide, "You speak French?" She only smiled and asked Babette to show her to their quarters.

The room had been completely redecorated since Nigel had returned. He employed decorators and personal shoppers to redo all of the master suites in less than a week. He wanted it to be perfect for her.

The master suite had been redone to be similar to her bedroom in New York and it even had the photo of the two of them above the bed. Good ole' Jessica. The coverlets, Babette said, had been changed to match her own and instinct had her check the bed, and true to form, the mattress was the same, soft on her side, and firm on his. She checked her closet space and there were several new items that still had tags on them that Nigel had purchased for her use while in Europe. Nice. Vanity's watched chimed.

Giles, tapped on the open-door frame and walked into the master suite. Vanity turned to find Nigel standing there watching her. "Dinner, is served," Giles announced.

Vanity wanted to know how capable Babette was and asked her to assist with putting her hair back up. Deft hands moved swiftly and created a French bun that was comfortable, fashionable, and easy to wear. "Oh, wow!" She hugged the girl before she knew it, saying, "Thank you, I love it." Babette grinned from ear to ear.

"Babette, can you excuse us?" Nigel asked, wanting to be alone with his wife.

The moment the door closed, Nigel moved to her, "This has been the longest week of my life. I thought you would never get here."

He planted small kisses on her face as she wrapped her arms around his waist and waited to receive the kiss she had been craving all week. Vanity wanted to tell him she felt the same way, but she had little time as he smothered her with affection.

BIDDIE SERVED A TRADITIONAL British dinner with entirely too much food, and Vanity pushed it around her plate. Initially she had thought to not offend the cook and at least try the food before she started bringing in her own, but it was difficult to consume the rich sauces and fried meats. But overall, dinner went well as Gianni discussed a few things he wanted to see while he was in Europe. As reluctant as Vanity was, she had to ask about his wardrobe, and as suspected, he only brought casual clothing. Her twin unfortunately, dressed like an out of work cowboy unless there was a cause for something special. He, also, unfortunately, entrusted Gianni with his fashion sense. Good thing she knew his sizes and sent a text to a friend to have suitable clothing sent over as soon as possible. They would be leaving for Strathmore Keep in the morning and she knew he needed to have a certain look for meeting the Duke and Duchess. She wasn't sure if the items he had brought would be proper enough.

Nigel could not resist the opportunity to poke fun at his wife, "Don't worry Gianni, she doesn't allow me to dress myself either."

{22} Scaling the castle walls...

In the daylight, Strathmore Keep was a great deal larger, more foreboding and it looked very cold. When Vanity had visited the castle earlier in the summer with her brother, Nigel had started a fire because he said it often got chilly inside the main hall. It was now a damp November, and the building was probably going to give her bronchitis.

The ride to the family estate and land was very pleasant as Nigel discussed some benefits of having such a great deal of property with Gianni. He also scowled as he spoke of the cost and upkeep of such a building.

"We try to maintain the historical significance of the structure, but the costs must also be factored in," Nigel said.

Gianni first looked out the window as they approached the massive stone tower, but then turned quickly to face Nigel, telling him, "You can compensate for the cost of heating and cooling by adding some well-placed solar panels. Adding small, inconspicuous wind turbines can increase the air flow throughout the building while recirculating fresh air, which greatly reduces staleness. It would also be beneficial to replace the standard water systems with low-flow shower heads and commodes which use solar generators," Gianni said to him with a confidence that Vanity had never seen before in her nephew.

"I know money may not be of any object, but conserving resources are always smart planning for the future," Gianni said to Nigel as he went back to gazing out of the window. "Ooh, is that a moat?"

Nigel stared at the kid in disbelief, amazed that one so young could be so attuned. Strathmore Keep was everything you would expect in a castle. Gianni could barely contain himself when Nigel assigned Giles' nephew to show him the estate and grounds.

"Careful around the south inner curtain you two. That wall is being reinforced," Nigel called after the young man that he was squiring. "Conall, make sure you take him into the garages." The young man nodded and Vanity was impressed at how well comported he was for someone so young.

"Is he a butler in training?" She asked her husband.

"Yes, he will be the butler for Collingswood, the Duke of Somerset," he said to Vanity with love in his eyes.

She arched one perfect eyebrow, "Who is Collingswood?"

Nigel pulled her into his arms, before kissing her, whispering, "Our son."

VANITY WAS ONLY SHOWN a portion of the castle since it had taken the better part of the morning to get there. Nigel's apartments were in the east wing of the Keep whereas his brother was in the west, his sister in the south, and his parents in the northeast corner. It amazed her that each compartment was self-contained with its own staff. Her watch chimed and before she even had an opportunity to say anything, a bell jingled on the door.

Nigel didn't bother to check the door, but guided her into a small eat-in area outside of the sitting rooms. A cute little table had been set with her midday meal, her bottles of water, and tea service for Nigel. Nice.

"Would you like to rest before meeting my parents this evening?" Nigel asked her as they concluded the meal.

"If at all possible, I need to get some work done. Is there Wifi and a place where I can set up? I will also need an extra chair for Gianni when he gets back if that is possible, Your Grace," she said it tongue-in-cheek as she watched his reaction.

"Of course, Darling, follow me," he guided her past the bedroom which completely took her breath away. The guest room she had shared before with her brother had been dark, with heavy wainscoting in oaks and the room boasted large antique furniture, heavy drapes, and brocade-covered walls that made the room feel more like a shrine to Henry the VIIIth than a home. However, Nigel's personal quarters had been softened with lavenders and soft teals with a pop of red in the middle of the bed. The curtains were heavy velvet in the Chinese red she loved to wear. Above the bed was a different photo of Nigel and her, the one of him dressed like an American tourist laughing as they boarded the roller coaster. The door which she thought led to closet actually opened into a replica of her New York office. It was complete with two mannequins and everything she had on her desk.

"I am speechless." Vanity said as her eyes misted and she felt her body begin to hum with excitement.

"Nigel, thank you, I," she tried to say as he pulled her into his arms and kissed her deeply.

"I will send Gianni your way," he said pulling away. "I have some things to prep before this evening, so if you will excuse me."

Wow, she mused. Nigel promised he would sweep her off her feet in a grand fashion. This is beyond amazing.

Vanity worked clear into the early portion of the afternoon, sending Gianni back out to hang with Conall, who brought a slew of emotions in Vanity's head and heart. That sixteen-year-old kid is being trained to the butler for their son. Our son. My son. What if the first child is not a boy? "No frickin' pressure there Nigel!"

It was then something very clear seeped into her heart. Vanity Devons wanted to be a mother.

BABETTE ARRIVED AN hour before dinner. "Madam, it is time for your bath," she said to Vanity, who watched the young woman with some interest. I hope she is not planning to give me one. Instead, she handed her clothing to Babette to be pressed while she quickly showered and donned under garments. Her hair was combed in a combination of loose curls that hung down her back and a tight bun atop her head. She opted for an-line navy velvet skirt with a mint green cardigan, white blouse, and navy pumps. Nigel looked for the trademark splash of red that Vanity Devons was known for, but instead, she went very conservative.

It wasn't what Nigel was expecting her to wear, but he approved.

"Darling, there is something I need to show you," he told her as he took her hand and guided her down a long hallway, down two corridors, and towards a deep set of stairs in the rear of the building's structure.

"If you want to make out in the dungeon, you can just stop right here, Your Grace," she rooted herself to the spot where she was standing and refused to move.

"Come Darling, you will like this. I promise," he told her as he slipped his hand into hers. Reluctantly, she followed along as Nigel walked up to a huge door with a hand print and retinal scanner. Maybe he is 007.

Vanity was trying not to frown, but for the third time in two weeks, her face was showing a great deal of expression, "What in the silk stockings is in there? The crown jewels?"

"Silk Stockings?"

She exhaled softly, "No self-respecting woman uses profanity to express her emotions. I choose other words to convey my sentiments."

"Uhmm...right then," he told her, knowing that what she was about to see would probably make her curse like a British sailor on holiday in Japan. He opened the large vaulted door and led her inside. The lights came up to reveal cases and cases of jewels. Some were in glass-doored containers that looked like safety deposit boxes, others were prominently displayed in trophy style cases. In the center aisles were softly illuminated crowns. "Each of these belonged to a duke or a duchess of Strathmore, some going back as far as the Tudors," he told her.

Vanity stood still, trying to take it all in. There were jewels in the vault to end world hunger forever.

"Darling, everything on the right side of the vault now belongs to you," Nigel told her.

Her forehead wrinkled, then her eyebrows shot up, and her ears got hot, "Say what now?"

Nigel laughed aloud, taking his wife into his arms, "After your coronation in the Spring, you will be given your own access codes to come down, take inventory, try on, play with, or auction off a piece if you so choose," he said. He took a small tablet from under a showing desk, "This is a list of every item in your inventory. I do caution you that the left side of the vault belongs to my mother and the back wall to my sister.

"That is a lot of bling," she whispered.

He asked her, "Darling, would you like to choose a piece or two to wear this evening?"

Vanity took the tablet from his hand and entered emeralds into the search engine. Photos showed up of every emerald piece in the vault. She wasn't quite certain how to navigate the system, "Nigel, how do I tell which pieces are your mother's or sisters?"

He showed and explained to her the codes. It only took her a matter of seconds to search again and find the perfect piece of jewelry for the evening. "Great, I would like to wear these," she told him.

{23] Meet the family...

"**I**s it true that Nigel actually flew to America to marry some tart who models undergarments?" Catherine Strathmore Howard asked her younger brother, Arthur.

"I heard she was some actress, but I am still trying to wrap my mind around our big brother getting on a plane to fly over the pond," Arthur said with some amusement.

Jane Parr Strathmore, Nigel's mother, told the siblings, "Do stop gossiping, you two. She must mean a great deal to him, otherwise he would not have even made the attempt. Besides, where are they? Dinner is about to start?"

Nigel Strathmore the III, with a glass of scotch in his hand and a cigar in his mouth spoke from the large recliner in the corner, told his wife, "He took her to the vault to make a jewelry selection for our dinner tonight."

Arthur was not going to miss an opportunity to make a jab at his brother, "Lovely. She is probably going to walk in wearing half of the pearls, a tiara, and the largest diamonds she could find."

Everyone was very surprised when Lady Wilhelmina entered the room to be presented to her husband's family, wearing only a pair of teardrop emerald earrings. Vanity remember her training and manners, performing a perfect curtsey in front of his parents and offering his brother and sister warm smiles.

"I would like to introduce to you my nephew Gianni, who will be working with me during the next week," she said to his family.

Arthur and Catherine were almost talking over each other, pelting her with questions about her trade, "I do say, I hear you are a lingerie model turned actress?"

"No, I am a model, who did some acting and I own a lingerie company," she responded politely. Arthur had more questions, but his attempt to be snarky was halted by the sounds of trumpeting fanfare.

Gianni leaned over to his aunt, "What is that?"

Vanity shrugged her shoulders, but Catherine answered the question. "It is the herald of the arrival of the Duke of Cambridge."

His eyes were wide as Gianni sprang up from the couch, "I need my camera. I need my phone. Can I take pictures of him, Your Grace? Will he allow me to take pictures with him?"

Vanity grabbed her nephew by the arm and pulled him back into the seat next to her, giving him a scolding glance.

Nigel was pretty droll about the whole scenario, "My cousin does like to make an entrance."

An informal receiving line was created as the Duke and Duchess of Cambridge arrived, with the duke making a beeline for Nigel. "I heard you had gotten married and I had to come in person to say hello."

As he faced Vanity, she performed another perfect curtsey for him and his wife.

"Your Highness," she said as she dipped low to greet them both. It was a shock to the entire room when the Duchess stepped forward, "Oh Vanity, do cut it out, six months ago you were measuring my tatas, and now you want to be formal?"

Catherine could not contain herself, "You know them?"

"Yes, she is one of my best clients," Vanity said.

THE FORMAL DINNER TURNED into an informal affair as the family moved to the common room where a very large grand piano sat in the middle of the floor. Vanity's heart leaped in her chest, "Is that a Blüthner, Style 9?"

Nigel asked her, "Would you like to favor us with a selection this evening, Lady Wilhelmina?"

Vanity's eyes shot to his parents, "May I? If it is okay. I would be honored to play for you."

Jane watched with interest as her daughter-in-law took a seat in front of the keys. Her fingers were shaking as they made contact with the coolness of the ivories and played her first note. Vanity closed her eyes as her fingers expertly maneuvered across the piano playing a Mozart standard, then segue into a

Chopin, and ending with a Bach. She played the last note and sat smiling at the keys, feeling warm on the inside.

"Darling, will you favor us with one more of your personal favorites," Nigel asked.

It was an easy choice as she began to play "Cry Me a River" but it was in her heart to begin to belt out the lyrics. Vanity closed her eyes as the words filled her lungs and the touch of the keys came to life under her fingers. The notes came from deep within the recesses of her soul. All the men who had tried to win her heart. All the lying men who had given empty promises to love and respect her, but to find out that she would not sleep with them. Bastards! She hit the keys hard. She threw her head back and bellowed out the notes. Her soprano filling the cavernous hall. The staff came from the kitchen to listen in the hallway.

Giles stood close by watching Nigel's face fill with pride as he watched his wife entertain his family. In truth, Giles, who stood listening, felt a connection to his Lordship's wife. Connall stood in the corner watching, feeling pride that she would produce the next heir to the Strathmore line. Jane, came to tears as she received a flashback of a young woman, who used to be her friend who loved to play as much as her daughter did as well. Wilhelmina Devonshire Strathmore was their Duchess. Each felt a sense of ownership and protectiveness of her. Nigel III, extinguished his cigar and watched with interest his son's choice of a wife and the producer of the next heir to his family line. He approved. His eldest, Nigel had made an excellent choice for a wife and mate.

The last key was struck. The air was crisp as the last notes came from her mouth a Capella closing out her mock recital. She finished and rose from the piano, so overwhelmed with emotion that she barely heard the applause. The Blüthner was at least 300 years old and perfectly tuned. Never had she imagined being able to play on anything so grand. Her body was humming as she felt something unlock within her midway through the song.

Vanity Devons could not appreciate the adoration that was being bestowed upon her. She was too busy being filled with sensations she had locked away for years.

IN THE QUIETNESS OF their bedroom, her body vibrated like a wayward guitar craving to be plucked. Each nerve in her was alive, awake, and energy was coursing through her.

"Nigel," she whispered into the darkened bedroom chamber.

There was no response as she moved closer to him.

"Stay on your side of the bed, Wilhelmina," came a voice from the other side of the massive bed. She ignored it and inched closer.

"Nigel," she said again as she reached out to feel the coolness of the sheets in the space between them, trying to locate the warmth of his body.

"Wilhelmina, stay on your side of the bed, please," he said again, this time sounding less convincing. It had been difficult when he saw her to not rip off the designer clothing and have his way with her, but a promise was a promise. If she moved any closer, he may not be able to keep his word.

She ignored his words when her fingers made contact with his arm, "That piano is marvelous. It was sitting there; just waiting for me to awaken it. Those keys came alive in my hands. It felt like energy bolts shot through my fingers." She told him as her fingers stroked his arm. "My whole body is infused with this humming, a strumming, a cry for more," her breathing was heavy.

Nigel tried to move away. *If she comes any closer, I may not be able to control myself.* Her piano playing and singing had turned him on to the point he had to leave the room after she played so he would not turn and inadvertently poke someone in the eye with his twig. "Darling, what are you doing?"

The covers were thrown to the side as she maneuvered her way through the bed and found his body. "I am just so warm all over, and the humming inside of me is like music, a Spanish guitar almost."

Nigel wondered if she was asleep. "Wilhelmina, wake up please."

"I'm very awake Nigel. My body is awake and I just need calm the frenzy," she told him as her hand reached into his sleep pants. She remembered what had worked for him in New York, and with a few quick flicks of her wrist, he was ready to aid her in calming the wayward notes that were soaring through her like free radicals. "I need to organize the notes, stop the humming, and make it all make sense."

"I don't understand, Darling. Tell me what you need," he asked as she climbed over him, straddling him.

She perfectly positioned him and began to gently rub her body against his. "I'm sorry, but I need the humming to stop," her mouth found his as she thrust her tongue in between his lips, still gently moving. "Help me Nigel. Help me compose this tune," she told him.

His hands went to her pajama top and released the snaps, freeing her breasts. He half rose and pulled one of the hardened buds into his mouth, which sent his wife in a tail spin. Vanity increased her pace as she grabbed a handful of his hair, increasing the rocking of her hips against him, "I can see the notes I can feel the music, I can hear it Nigel." She leaned forward, rocking faster, harder, quicker, kissing him once more and then collapsed in his arms.

"Wilhelmina, are you awake?" Nigel asked worried that me may have married a nutter.

Soft fingers touched his face, "I am."

"That was quite lovely, but what in the bloody hell was that about?"

Her breathing was ragged as she tried to find the words to explain her wanton actions, "I could hear the music and it felt like it was trapped inside me, I had to set it free."

"Is the music free now?"

"Yes, you helped me get the music out."

Nigel was quiet for a second, "What about me? I can feel a song trapped inside my trousers."

Vanity placed her hands under the covers and reached for him, but he stopped her with his words, "No, not this time. You got a chance to rub one out, I deserve the same." Even in the dark, she could feel the intensity of his stare.

"Nigel, really, are we going to go tit for tat?"

"Yes, we are, Darling," he told her as he reached for her in the darkness, pressing his body close and covering her mouth with his own as he gently rubbed himself against her, trying desperately to be calm, when in his heart he wanted to remove all of their clothing and actually make love to his wife. A step at a time, Nigel.

"Wrap your legs around me, Wilhelmina, help me make the music of love," he said as in the dark, they moved together, composing a tune that only they could hear.

NIGEL STOOD AT THE back door with Conall discussing the upcoming week at his country estate. He would return to his quarters shortly to check on his wife, but he had asked the young man to come along as a companion to Gianni since the two had managed to form an instant connection. He had been very impressed with Gianni's ideas and looked forward to the next few days of talking with him.

"There you are, my dear," his mother Jane said. "I was hoping to have a moment alone with you before you left for the country."

Startled that she had managed to walk up on him without him hearing her, Nigel greeted his mother warmly with an embrace followed by a kiss on her temple. "Good morning Mum."

"Will you join me straight away in my office?" Nigel followed along behind his mother, grabbing a few grapes from the fruit bowl on the kitchen counter and popping them in his mouth.

His mother's office was in the rear of the Keep. It was a moderately sized space with lots of windows that brought in as much natural light one could expect from a late fall season in England. The office was organized with materials from social functions, the charities she supported, and the running Strathmore Keep. The country house in Gloucester was going to be the responsibility of his wife as well as the London Townhome. He made a mental note to have a discussion with his wife of where and how they wished to reside. The one thing was clear, he did not want to live in Strathmore Keep. He hated the castle.

Jane patted the overstuffed chair that sat next to her desk, encouraging her son to take a seat. He recognized the Stamford wing chair that she had reupholstered after finding it in the root cellar behind some vintage wines. It was his favorite chair in the whole castle. "I have never had to worry about you Nigel," she said to him as her eyes began to tear.

"You have always been an ideal child. Never a problem, always doing what was expected of you, your title, and the Strathmore name."

The sound of the start of the conversation bristled Nigel a bit, and he only asked, "But..."

Jane dabbed at her eyes with an embroidered silk handkerchief, "I have always been worried that you would marry someone who was appropriate and fitting your station, but you would not marry for love." She leaned forward and grabbed his hands, "I am so proud of you Nigel. You managed as always to get it just right."

She rose and pulled him into her arms, squeezing him tightly. "Your wife is absolutely lovely. I cannot wait to get to know her better."

Always the good son, he squeezed her back. "I am glad you feel that way, Mum. I have a major favor to ask of you." He gave her a full-on smile that a son gives to his mother when he wants to borrow the car or a wad of cash.

She knew the look as her blue eyes gazed back at him, "What can I help you with son?"

"I would like the wedding and coronation to be here at Strathmore Keep in April," he waited for her reaction.

His mother clutched her bosom. Her eyes were wide in disbelief, "That is only six months away! Six months, Nigel? For a wedding and a coronation?"

It was the perfect opportunity to poke fun at her, "Of course, if it is too much trouble Mum, I can hire someone to handle the particulars."

"You will do no such thing," she said as she began to thumb through her desk looking for her planner. "Off with you now, I have so much to do. I will be out to the manor in a day or so. Please tell your wife to expect me."

Nigel held his mother in his arms, kissing her on the forehead, "Thank you Mum. I love you."

Jane heard nothing he said as her mind began filling with details to make this the best wedding of the social season.

{24] Are those Arabians...?

The morning was quiet. Vanity sat in the middle of the bed with her arms wrapped around her knees feeling foolish. Uncertain of how she was going to face her husband this morning after her behavior last night, she tried deep breathing, but the dread was hovering around her like guilt about eating a whole box of Krispy Kreme doughnuts. Couple that feeling with being insanely hungry, alongside a lightheadedness which was throwing her off-kilter. The bell chimed and she knew Giles had brought up some food. As much as she wanted to eat what had been placed before her last night, she could not consume the heavy sauteed foods and meats floating in onions and dark liquors. It was also a 21-course meal. Who still does that? It was a conscious decision not to draw attention to her different eating needs. She opted instead to just push the food around her plate, nibbling at the shellfish course, bypassing the consommé's and thick soup course.

Nigel entered the room carrying a towel and giving her a bird's-eye view of his naked bum as he adjusted the flame on the gas fireplace in the bedroom.

"Good Morning, Darling. I hope you slept well. I am absolutely famished."

It was good to see him in great spirits, but Vanity was still feeling stupid. He slipped on a pair of loungers and a tee and she could hear him pouring himself a cup of tea. She had not moved from the bed. "Wilhelmina, I know you are starving, you barely ate anything last night."

Slowly, she climbed down from the giant bed and made her way to the small table to join him for breakfast. "What's wrong, Darling? You seem out of sorts. Do I need to ring for a physician?"

"Nigel, it's about last night..."

He said nothing as he watched the emotions flicker through her eyes and when she looked up at him, he immediately recognized she felt shame for last night.

"Why are you upset this morning my love?"

"I behaved badly last night and I am sorry. I did not comport myself as I should have," she said with her head lowered.

In his head, there were so many ways to tackle this, but he took the issue head on, "Yes, you are right. If you had done it the right way, we both would have been naked and it would have lasted a lot longer."

Vanity's head popped up and her jaw hung open in shock. Nigel was chuckling over his teacup. She asked, "You aren't ashamed of me?"

"I am ashamed that I didn't do a better job getting you out of those clothes, but I promised you I would give you time, and I am," he said as he wiggled his brows and bit into a scone.

"Nigel, be serious! I came at you like a strumpet in heat and dry humped you all the way to Happy Town!"

"Yes, and the town needs a new Constable because I want to file a complaint," he said to her while still chuckling. Vanity threw a scone at him.

She wanted to know, "What do you have to complain about?"

"It could have been so much better if you had given me a chance to help you more," he said looking at her with a deliciously wicked grin.

She found herself blushing. "I mean, we are grown people, and here I am carrying on like a teenager with all of these sex hang-ups."

He took a few moments to gather his thoughts by slicing into the Eggs Benedict and taking a mouthful, followed by the washing it down with his tea. "Darling, we said we were going to date a bit before we moved forward with anything more."

"Yes, well..."

"We are doing what people do when they date; regardless of age. I mean, it was lovely, and I don't wish to make a habit of it, but we are getting there. And we have time," he said as he added a spot of jam to a corner of his scone.

A nibble at her pineapple showed him she was not convinced. Nigel said, "You also seem to be missing two very important points, Darling." Her eyes asked what are those?

"In both instances, you initiated intimacy with me," he told her as realization showed on her face. "And both times were after you played the piano." He looked up at her. "You do know what this means don't you?"

She shook her head no. Nigel's face was stern as he told her, "It means that I am going to ask you to play something every night before bed, first thing in the morning, before the midday meal," he paused her effect, "which will make me the official G'Vnah of Happy Town."

Her husband had pointed out something that she never realized that maybe her passion tied to playing the piano? Nigel also discovered something else as well. she was not frigid.

This was going to change things a great deal.

THE RIDE TO THE COUNTRY estate was filled with Nigel having a conversation with Gianni about his ideas for making the property greener. The hour's ride to Gloucester left Vanity with an overwhelming sense of helplessness. Her underbelly had been exposed and she was terrified that her husband would use it to his advantage. She eyed him in the passionate conversation with Gianni and a lascivious thought seeped into her mind.

He can tickle my underbelly anytime.

Oftentimes when her models would stay over, they would speak of mindblowing sexual experiences, assuming she had shared similar times with Joe. Few people knew that Joe, the famous Mr. Hollywood Blockbuster himself, was gay. The past four years she had served as his beard, pretending to be something they were not.

Last night, the real woman in her had been awakened and she liked it. The idea of rolling over on her husband and relieving herself had felt amazing. His mouth on her breast had awakened a beast inside of her.

I can only imagine what it is going to be like to feel him inside me. She was staring at him in a way that brought his attention to her face.

"Wilhelmina, did you hear me? You seem lost in your own head over there."

"I'm sorry, Nigel. What did you say?"

He opened the car door and stepped out, taking her by the hand and pulling her out his side of the rear door, "I said 'Welcome home.'"

The country manor estate was everything she had imagined it to be. A Tudor-styled brick manor house that probably served as some love nest for one of his ancestors. As they walked down the drive, she and Gianni were hit with a familiar scent.

"I smell horses?" Gianni asked first.

But before Nigel could answer, both his wife and her nephew made a bee-line toward the back of the house, following the smell until they found the stables. "Are those Arabians?"

"Yes, I have four Arabians, a couple of Shire horses, a spotted pony that we used for rides for the kids during summer fairs, and a Welara. This home is a sport house used for hunting."

Both Vanity and Gianni's heads snapped around while simultaneously asking, "What do you hunt?"

"Quail, grouse, the occasional rabbit for winter stews," he said cautiously. "Mainly, we ride and grow vegetables, and I mostly shoot clays. It has served as more of a getaway from the city and a place where I can think than anything."

His words were moot and aimed at the back of their heads once the barn doors were opened and they saw the horses. "May we ride?" Gianni asked Nigel.

"Of course. Lady Wilhelmina, do you ride as well?"

Her eyes were sparkling as she approached the jet-black Arabian that seemed to lower his head in respect to the lady.

Nigel turned his back to look for a groomsman or a stable boy, "I will get someone to saddle a horse for you." He walked out the side door to find Hamish, the stable master, only to return and find the horses saddled and his wife climbing aboard a very spirited animal he saved only for seasoned riders. He called to her but she had mounted up and taken off down meadow.

Gianni mounted the Walera, "No worries Your Grace, I will catch up to her."

Nigel's heart was thudding in his chest as he urged Hamish to saddle him a ride, but he remained standing where he was, watching the braid of his wife's hair ripple in the wind. She made it to the top of the crest when the horse reared up and Vanity disappeared from the saddle.

{25} M'Lady...M'Lady

The wind stopped blowing, the sun stopped shining, and angels in heaven had fallen to earth in Nigel's eyes as he grabbed the first horse available, minus the saddle, and went galloping in the direction he had seen his wife fall. Gianni was ahead of him, putting his horse through the paces as he rode hard towards the crest. Nigel prayed aloud, begging, please Dear Heavenly Father, don't let her be hurt. He also prayed silently as his hands clung to the mane of the horse. Midway through the meadow, he saw the shadow upon the crest and his wife seated upon the horse. Her braid had come loose and the hair flowed behind her and she rode hard towards the manor.

Had he not been scared out of his mind, Nigel would have believed it was the most beautiful vision he'd ever seen in his whole life. Gianni had already turned his horse, following along behind his aunt who was holding something in one hand and the reins in the other. In the distance a bell rang and the keepers of the manor gathered at the back of the house to aid in whatever call of need was signaled by the sounding of the Strathmore Bell.

Biddie, Giles, Babette, Conall, and Hamish were waiting at the back door when Vanity rode up on the horse, carrying a small child in her arms. "Nigel, she came out of nowhere! I didn't see her and she spooked the horse."

The dark-haired child with the large blue eyes looked at everyone in fear that she would be punished.

"Are you okay, sweetie?" Vanity asked as she checked the child for bruises, cuts, and sprains. "Where are your parents?"

Conall spoke up, "She lives down the way a bit, in the village. I think her name is Lisbane, M'Lady."

"Babette, it seems we both need to be cleaned up a bit. Will you assist us?" Vanity's hair had made some new friends, as she now sported leaves and twigs in her tresses. The child who could have been no more than five years old, said, "I am hungry. Can I have something to eat?"

"Of course, but first let's wash your face and hands," Vanity said as she looked at Babette, who quickly secured a soapy wet cloth. With delicate care and ease, Vanity washed the child's face, taking extra care with the scrapes.

"Biddie, where is the bread?" she asked as looked around the huge country kitchen, trying to sort out where she thought the food stores may be kept.

From the fridge she grabbed a whole ham and lobbed off a chunk, sliced off a wedge of cheese, and cored an apple. Nigel watched as she made a plate of food for the child that ended up having a happy face with apple smiles, and grape eyes. It was a delight to the child who nibbled at the fruit, looking at Vanity as if she were a fairy with magical wings.

"You are pretty. I like your hair," she said as she crunched on the apple.

"You are pretty as well. What is your name?"

"Lisbane...Annie Bersky."

Vanity looked at Conall, who understood the unspoken command, "Yes, M'Lady, right away."

It was then that Vanity looked down at herself. She was covered in mud, her coat was torn, and she had scraped the side of her face. The skin was broken and she was three days away from a show.

"I am a mess," she said and she noticed Hamish standing there. Although they had not been introduced formally, based on what he was wearing, she knew him to be the stable master. "Your name, good sir?" She asked.

"I am Hamish, M'Lady, the stable master."

She patted at her hair, "Normally, I would return my own horse and brush it down, but as you can see, I shall be detained a bit and I do not want the animal to sit. Will you be so kind and take care of it for me this one time?"

"It is my job, M'lady. You will never have to do that," he said, shocked that she would even want to do it herself.

As she walked closer to the stable master, he took a step back when she told him, "I was always taught to put away my toys. If I take it out, it's my responsibility to put it away." She stepped around him and went outside to the horse, feeding it an apple. "Next time, my lovely, we will have a much longer ride."

The reins were handed to Hamish as she walked back inside. "Nigel, which way is our quarters?"

He stood shocked, trying to compose himself. Thoughts ran through his head. He was certain if he wanted to kiss her or strangle her. It amazed him that Wilhelmina acted as if she hadn't just scared the living shit out of me.

Calm and poised, he pointed towards the stairs. Once she opened a few doors, she would immediately know which room was theirs. Vanity looked at Babette, "I will be back shortly." Then she thought about it a bit, and went back over to Lisbane, "I will be back in a jiff, Little One."

"You sound funny when you talk!" Lisbane told her with a scrunched up little nose that Vanity touched with the tip of her finger.

She followed Nigel to the master suite and headed right for the shower. The warm water ran through her hair as she closed her eyes, letting the liquid slow her rapidly beating heart. I was so scared. She jumped when she heard the shower door open and her nude husband stepped in with her.

"Nigel what are you doing?"

"What does it look like," he said as he reached for her and pulled her into his arms. "For a second there, my heart stopped beating. When that horse reared up and you disappeared, I thought my world had ended." He wiped away the wet strands of her hair. "I am so in love with you, Wilhelmina, that I could not imagine my life without you. Don't ever scare me like that again."

"Nigel," she said in a low voice as she draped her arms about his waist. "It is only a scrape. I am okay."

"But I am not," he held her tighter. "We can't grow old together if you keep stopping my heart."

He said nothing more while doing nothing less than sharing the joy that she had not been hurt or killed.

NIGEL SAT QUIETLY IN front of the fire in the master suit. Vanity was dressed and downstairs checking on the child. He was lost in his own thoughts when Giles entered the room to bring him a change of clothing for the afternoon. It was an odd relationship between the two because Giles was family to him. They had basically grown up together, with the butler being only 15 years older than Nigel. The man served Nigel as a butler, a confidant, and an unspoken friend. However, both were careful to never cross the line of the very distinctive roles each held with the other.

He brought Nigel a clean pair of hunting boots and placed them beside his feet. It was the hesitation that made his Lordship look up at his longtime right hand, "Is something wrong Giles?"

Nose in the air, posture upright, Giles cleared his throat, "permission to speak freely Your Grace?"

Nigel rose to face him, "Of course, always Giles." He held his breath. This was uncommon for his butler to offer an opinion unless requested.

"With all due respect Your Grace," he paused. "I would have crossed an ocean and half a continent to collect her as well. I speak on behalf of the staff, including myself, we have fallen in love with Lady Wilhelmina."

He cleared his throat again, bowed his head and turned to leave. "Giles," Nigel called after him.

"Yes, Your Grace?"

Nigel walked over to him and uncharacteristically, threw his arms around the man and hugged him. "Thank you. It means a lot to hear you say that."

"Good day, Your Grace."

{26} What are you thinking...

It was a quiet ride into the village that surrounded the manor. Not much had changed in the small farming town that was overseen by the Duke. The quaint village was well known for its cheeses and something else that was becoming prevalent, crystal meth. As quickly as the constable shut down an operation, another popped up like an irreverent game of Whack A Mole.

Once she had gotten cleaned up, she met Lisbane in the kitchen to chat with her why she was out in the middle of a field. "I was hungry and picking some berries."

"You were quite a long way from home. I know your Mum is going to be really scared," Vanity told her as she double-checked the pony tails that Babette had put on the little girl's head.

"They won't miss me. I leave every day to go and look for food because we don't have any," Lisbane said as she placed a chunk of bread in her pocket. Most of the staff had returned to the kitchen and were listening in to see how the Duke's new wife would handle the child. Vanity loaded a shopping bag with sundries and half a pot roast to take home with the little girl. A home that that turned out to be not fit for living, even by the vast quantities of vermin that had taken over the cottage.

"I was wonderin' where ya had gotten off, ya little skamp," a woman with dirty black hair said to the child as they walked up to the door. Vanity did not stop as she walked up to the front door, waiting to be invited inside. The lady looked up to see Nigel standing there, "Pardon me, Your Grace, I dinna see ya standing there. Was my little Lisbane a botherin' ya?"

"No, madam, she was nearly trampled by a horse, though, so we thought we would bring her home," Nigel told the woman as he handed her the sack of goods. "The little one seemed to take a fancy to this beef roast, so I sent some home with her. I hope you don't mind."

"No we don't mind at all, yer Grace," she said as she took the bag. Her eyes went back to Vanity, who was kneeling in front of Lisbane.

"You know where to find me Sweetie," Vanity told Lisbane, giving the little girl a squeeze.

"Bye, M'Lady," Lisbane said as Nigel pulled Vanity by the arm towards the car.

They drove back in silence, but he could almost hear the buzzers going off in her head "What are you thinking?" He already knew, but he was not prepared to have another Phan incident on his hands.

"Her mother is a drug addict and that house is not fit for even the mice to live in," she told him.

"Yes, but they are her parents and are doing the best they can for her in their current state," Nigel responded keeping his eye on the road.

Vanity understood something far deeper than Nigel ever would—drug addicts only cared about themselves, "No, my husband, they are doing the best they can for themselves. In a few months, they will have her stealing for them and after that, maybe worse."

Uncertain of what to say once they arrived back at the manor, the conversation about little Lisbane was replaced with the preparation for the arrival of Jessica and Clarke tomorrow. There was still so much to get done in a few days. She was due in Milan in less than four days with a show to put on in less than a week, but her mind kept wandering back to the child, realizing with a great deal of certainty that they wouldn't even miss her.

Nigel came around the corner and popped his head into the downstairs office off of the kitchen that he had created for his wife. "The answer is no!" he exclaimed.

She turned in the chair, smiling sweetly at him, "What are you going on about, Your Grace?"

"I am speaking about what is going through that pretty head of yours. No, she is not yours, she cannot be yours, and no, you can't stick her in your suitcase on the way to Milan." He kissed the top of her head and headed out the back door to mount his horse to ride with Gianni to review some options for the property.

If there was one thing Vanity Devons understood, what is fated for you to have eventually will come to fruition. Whether it be a husband, an unborn child with an already trained butler, or a beautiful child in need of a home. What is meant to be, shall be.

THE CRISP NOVEMBER wind blew into the partially opened window as Vanity Devons looked below at the rolling meadow, once green, but now brown in its fall slumber. In a few short months, the rains would come and hydrate the sleeping fields and new life would begin again. Lisbane deserved a new life. Yet in her heart, she knew her life with Nigel was complicated enough, and there were still issues to be addressed that she had yet to broach.

For Pete's Sake, I haven't even consummated my marriage. More importantly, I have to figure out how to move Vanity Devons to Europe.

A gentle knock came to the door and Vanity assumed it was Babette coming to do her hair, but instead, she was informed she had a visitor. It was only 7:30 am. Who could be calling on her this early in the morning? His heart raced as she jammed her feet into a soft pair of leather loafers and bounded down the stairs. She hadn't bothered to bind her hair, allowing it to flow behind her as she descended the stairwell. In the front foyer, there stood a five-year-old Lisbane, still wearing the same dirty clothing she had on yesterday.

The girl made an attempt at a curtsey, "Good morning, M 'Lady."

Vanity looked to Babette then at Giles, who spoke for them both, "She arrived alone, M 'Lady."

Taking to one knee, Vanity addressed the child, "Have you snuck away again Lisbane?"

As if from her mouth to God's ear the child responded, "They are not going to miss me. I was hoping," Lisbane said, twirling her fingers in the dirty frock she wore.

Vanity said nothing as she stared into the small blue eyes that begged for acceptance as she asked, "I was hoping that maybe there is something I could help you with today. I'm good with chores. Me Mum ate most of the food. The mice got into the rest."

Slowly, Vanity rose to her feet and placed her hands on her hips. She gave Giles a look, then Babette, before letting her eyes go back to the child. "I am not sure Lisbane, I have an extremely busy day today."

"I am a good helper, M 'Lady. I can sweep and dust," the child said.

Vanity eyed the dirty face and grimy hair, "Okay, but first, you have to get cleaned up."

"Like a bath?" Lisbane asked as she started walking towards the door she came in, trying to leave.

She saw Giles turn his head to keep from laughing. "Yes, a bath. Your hair washed and trimmed, those teeth scrubbed, as well as the rest of you."

"Well, that's not fair!" Lisbane said with a stomp of her little foot.

Vanity turned and headed towards the stairs, "Giles, please see that Lisbane gets home safely."

Lisbane's little eyes were wide, "Wait, M'Lady. Only one bath though!"

Vanity came back and kneeled in front of the child, offering the little girl a handshake, "Deal!"

However, before she asked Babette to give the child a thorough bath and homemade delousing, she inquired if the Duke had any spare fabric on hand that she could use. "Of course, M'Lady, follow me," Giles told her as they headed towards Nigel's home office.

In a closet in the back of the room were bolts of unused fabrics. "Giles, do you think your Lordship would mind me taking a yard or two from these cotton bolts?"

"These bolts were sent here as samples that I will either ship to a wholesaler or discounter in the East End," Giles said, still curious as to how she was going to use the material, but his facial expression asked, 'what are you thinking?'

"Last thing, Giles, and I will leave you to your duties. I need an old cotton pillowcase," she told him.

Scissors, fabric, and pillowcase in hand, she went to her new home office that looked exactly like her office in New York, all the while asking Babette to bring the child. She measured twice, cut once, and from the pillowcase she made a pattern for a chemise for Lisbane. Vanity used the same pattern to cut a small under slip from the pink cotton fabric she found in Nigel's office, fashioning a pair of matching pink bloomers. She used some light wool to fashion a jumper and a yard and a half of light blue cotton to make a light long sleeve slip on shirt. Biddie located a small roll of lace, and she watched in earnest as the Duke's wife made a perfect outfit for the little girl, trimming both the dress and bloomers with lace.

The entire staff was buzzing, and it only got louder when they heard a plane flying overhead and the doorbell chimed, heralding the arrival of Lady Jayne Strathmore. On top of everything else, she had to do today, along with the coming of Jessica, Clarke, and boxes of lingerie, Nigel's mother had made an unannounced visit.

I can handle this. Just a step at a time.

{27} Time for tea...

The small dress in hand, Vanity rounded the corner to greet her mother-in-law, who was smartly dressed in a two-piece skirt and jacket with a matching fall hat. It was then that Vanity realized her hair still had not been combed, and her black slacks had picked up lint from the pink cotton she was working with to make the undies for her special little guest. A guest that decided she didn't want a bath after all. Vanity spotted a little pink naked bum poking out from under a table as Babette apologized profusely while trying to pull the child towards her.

Vanity pretended she saw none of it, "Lady Jayne, what an unexpected surprise."

Jayne was trying to process a random naked child running around her son's home, but was too taken aback when a tall Hispanic man wearing pink pearls and a fuchsia fascinator walked in the door. Well, walked wasn't the word since Clarke considered himself to be a more of a glider than a stepper.

He greeted Vanity with a European approach by kissing both of her cheeks before launching into a tirade. "I swear, Honey, between your cousin's flying and your nephew's driving, I nearly became straight before having a heart attack and going to meet my maker." He clutched at the pearls and noticed Jayne standing in the foyer. "And who is this delightful doll of a duchy?"

Vanity tried to reel him in, but it was too late. Clarke had been unleashed.

"Clarke, Jessica, this is Nigel's mother, the Duchess of Strathmore," she said as she introduced both Jessica and Clarke. Jayne gasped as she watched the colorful man in the colorful clothing perform a perfect, colorful curtsey.

Clarke walked up to her, "Please tell me I get to do a makeover on you, Girl, and update that do, and create an ever more glam you!"

This time Jayne clutched her pearls. Jessica pinched Clarke and a naked Lisbane ran by giggling.

"Who is that naked white child?" Clarke asked with his necked pulled back and face contorted like he smelled an anomalous fart.

"That is Lisbane, and if you can catch her, I would like to put these clothes on her I just made," Vanity said.

With a shrug of his shoulders, Clarke sauntered after the child calling, "Here little naked white girl." He called her as if he was calling the family dog from the back yard. "Here little white child, come here, Pumpkin."

By this point, Babette had stopped chasing Lisbane and was too preoccupied watching Clarke.

Jessica, who was always all business, asked, "Where is the office?"

Vanity pointed toward the kitchen and as her eyes looked up, she was shocked to see her brother David, followed by Chuck, Gianni, and a very furious Nigel, who seemed to be in a heated argument with Chuck.

"I am not sure why in the bloody hell you thought it would be okay to land a plane in a farming community!"

"I didn't hit a sheep or anything, 006," Chuck said as he spotted Babette.

"Who gave you permission to land a plane here, anyway?" Nigel wanted to know.

"Gianni gave me the coordinates and the clearance," Chuck said as he walked over to Babette and kissed her hand, causing the woman to blush.

"And why are you listening to him? Last I checked, the property belonged to me," Nigel's face had started to turn red. Gianni chose this time to throw in his two cents.

"Your Grace, I found a barouche trail in the back fields that was still clear and in perfect working condition. It is long enough for Lady Wilhelmina's plane to land. There is even enough room for an aided turn around for takeoff." He said it so calmly that it actually calmed Nigel, but in the same sentence, Gianni turned to Biddie, "Ooh, is that pie?"

As Biddie handed him a large slice, Gianni turned back to Nigel. "It is actually larger and longer than the landing strip at our house."

Nigel's eyes were wide, "You have a landing strip for a plane at your house? Your Dad must sell a lot of books."

Gianni bobbed his head yes, adding, "And a helipad for Big Daddy's helicopter. But my dad had White Bear build the landing strip for Willie. I mean Lady Wilhelmina's plane."

It was all overwhelming Nigel, "Your grandfather has a helicopter? What is a White Bear?"

Conall was amazed by everything he was hearing and asked, "Do you live in one of those fancy big American mansions?"

Gianni shook his head no, "I live on a ranch and White Bear is an Indian. He kind of came with the ranch."

Nigel had never bothered to ask how the kid knew so much and understood now. "Wait, you live on a ranch? Your dad owns a ranch? Hold up, what kind of Indian?"

Chuck didn't want to be left out, "An American Indian and yes, that's right, I land that plane on some smaller and tighter spaces than your little duchy here, 005!"

In the middle of all the chaos, David was focused on his sister, "Hello, Vain one," he embraced her fully with a big kiss on her cheek. She in turn introduced him to Nigel's mother, who fanned herself as David performed a regal bow over her hand, giving it a delicate kiss. "I am honored to make your acquaintance," he said with a glimmer in his eye.

Jayne clutched at her pearls again as a naked Lisbane ran by again giggling, this time with Clarke behind her yelling and gliding across the floor like an apparition, "Little naked white girl, I am tired of chasing you. Now get on over here!"

Nigel was still fuming at Chuck, who had been decreasing the James Bond secret service clearance since his arrival from 007 down to 002, and the last insult, Nigel had reached his limit, especially when Chuck said, "Calm down Mr. Bean, it's not like I ran over one of your sheep for your mutton stew or anything."

It was difficult to tell if Nigel was amused or fit to be tied. He removed his cap and threw it to the floor, "Mr. Bean? Mr. Bean? That's it, Charles, I am going to kick your arse!"

Chuck was tickled by the whole thing, "Oh, so we are formal now are we? It's Charles now, eh, Mate?"

Nigel took off running at Chuck, who took off out the back door. Lisbane made her last pass and David reached down and scooped her up. "It seems that my sister has made you a rather pretty frock, but you must get cleaned up to put it on." David spotted Babette, who had stopped staring at Clarke and was now staring at David, who politely placed the child in her arms. He removed the little dress and cute underpants from his sister's hand and also gave those to Babette. "Be quick little one, so we can have tea."

Clarke flopped down at the table. His fascinator had come detached from his head and hung in the middle of his forehead like a bright fuchsia pimple. "Dear Lord, fetch the smelling salts 'cause a queen's about to faint from heart palpitations!"

Lisbane was ecstatic to have tea with so many people as she and Babette made their way up the stairs, her little white bum peeking out from between Babette's arms. Nigel came in the back door covered in dirt and Chuck's bottom lip was poked out. Vanity looked closely at his face and appeared as if her cousin had been socked in the eye.

"Willie, Nigel hit me," Chuck confessed. He plopped down at the table in a sulking fit as Biddie ran to fetch ice for the swelling eye.

Nigel was quick to point out, "Well, he hit me first. What do you have to say now Charles? That you got your arse kicked by Mr. Bean?"

Suddenly, with his mouth pursed to say the next words, Nigel stopped as if he had just stumbled into a den of hungry lions. Slowly he turned his upper body to locate his wife in the room, locating her person and locking his eyes with hers. He blinked several times as if he were adjusting the blue eyes.

He asked, in an accusatory tone, "Wait... did I see a naked child running through here earlier?"

Everyone in the room turned to look at Vanity, who gave her husband a radiant smile.

It didn't work.

Nigel raised his voice to her, "Wilhelmina! Did you steal that child?"

Vanity's mouth popped open as if she were waiting to catch popcorn treats being thrown across the room. Her voice, full of indignation and her hands propped on her hips, "Nigel, how could you think I would do such a thing?"

Chuck lowered the ice pack from his eye, "Did she tell you about the time she stole the duck from the petting zoo?"

David, not to be left out added, "Or the time she stole the monkey from the actual zoo?"

Jessica had made it back into the area where everyone was, "well, she stole me from Diddy, in the middle of Fashion Week; during the fashion show, I might add."

Vanity's mouth was still opened wide in disbelief. All eyes turned to Clarke, who was brutally honest as always and contributed, "Oh she didn't steal me, Honeys. She walked by the salon where I was working on the Upper East Side and I packed up my grip and followed her home! I was like a little lost puppy boy."

Vanity was outdone. She looked at Giles, who was standing there doing his best to contain his laughter. "Giles, would you be so kind and tell my husband that I have not left this house!"

Giles, back straight and looking at his boss, "It is true Your Grace. She has not left the estate. The child showed up this morning asking to break her fast with the Lady."

Vanity raised both her hands, "See!"

Nigel was so frustrated he couldn't see straight, "And where did you get the clothes for the child that were in your hand a minute ago?

"I just made those, Husband."

"Out of what?"

"Giles gave me some fabric from your office."

Giles mouth popped open in shock that she was so willing to throw him under the bumpy barouche that was whizzing past. "M' Lady!"

Vanity poked her tongue out at him and Giles almost recoiled at the unladylike action and her words to him, "I'm not going down alone, Buddy!" Giles tried to say something, but instead the only sounds that came from his mouth sounded like a little Pomeranian trying to jump up on a couch.

It was in the midst of all the chaos that a beautiful sound was heard that caused everyone in the room to stop. At first it sounded like a snort. Then a chortle followed by a rousing, belly gut laugh. Jayne had taken a seat at the table to take everything in and found the whole scenario to be totally amusing. This is also when Nigel realized his mother was in the room, "Oh my, Mum, I didn't know you were here."

"It is fine, son. It has been a long time since this house was filled with so much warmth and laughter," she dabbed at the corner of her eyes with a handkerchief. Vanity's watch chimed and right on cue, Biddie entered with a tray of tea, scones, and Vanity's food.

As if she was saved by the bell, Vanity said "I guess that settles it then;everyone wash up. The tea is ready."

{28} Making preparations...

It was amazing that after all the rigmarole, the rest of the day settled in nicely. There was the minimal swelling to Chuck's eye and Biddie cooked up an amazing full breakfast for everyone to enjoy. It seemed that Lisbane was enjoying herself more than anyone, relishing in the attention being paid to her in the new warm frock with matching bloomers. The lace made her feel pretty and made the little girl inclined to pull up the back of her dress to show everyone her new pink pretties.

Nigel, freshly showered and hair still damp, returned to the table. First, he gave his mother a kiss on the cheek. Next, a warm kiss to his wife, and Lisbane stood on the chair waiting for hers as well. Nigel bent down and gave the little girl a raspberry on her forehead, which sent her into a fit of giggles. Finally, it was Chuck who asked many wanted to know.

"So, Lady Wilhelmina," He paused, making a point of getting her title correct while giving Nigel the evil eye. "What's up with the kid?"

This topic caught the attention of Lady Jayne, who looked at Wilhelmina, "I didn't want to prod my Dear, but I too am curious about the child."

Vanity shrugged her shoulders, "I nearly killed her yesterday with the horse I was riding. She came out of nowhere. We took her home last night, but she came back this morning."

Seeing the questions in Lady Jayne's face prompted Vanity to continue speaking, "I can imagine it is tough to be a parent, especially with a willful child, but every kid deserves to live in a safe environment and have their parent's as protectors."

"Did you find her parents unbecoming, Lady Wilhelmina?" Jayne asked.

It was not an easy answer to give, but Vanity tried her best to explain her thoughts, "I have yet to be a mother and I know my trials and tribulations are ahead of me, so I find myself to be in no position to judge."

Lady Jayne held onto her tea cup, watching the interaction between her daughter-in-law and the child as she demonstrated the proper way to apply cream to her scone, but not partaking of one herself. "Based on what I have heard this morning Lady Wilhelmina, you seem to be an advocate of rescuing what is in harm's way. Will that be your platform; child advocacy and animal rights?"

"At this stage Lady Jayne, I can only advocate what is pressing for me and to me. And that is my marriage and starting a family."

With the words spoken aloud, every head at the table turned to her. She even realized that a few ears were probably listening in the kitchen.

Jayne pressed her hands to her bosom, "Oh my, that is exciting news!"

Vanity reached across the table and touched her hand, "Not quite yet, Lady Jayne," she said as she gave Nigel a very provocative look that caused him to stop chewing. "But soon, hopefully very soon."

Nigel began choking as David jumped up to pat him in the back. Vanity acted as if she had said nothing untoward and spoke to Jayne, "So, what is the nature of your visit today?"

"Oh Dear! I got so caught up in the excitement. I came to speak with you about the wedding and coronation."

Nigel jumped up from the table, "David, Chuck, and Gianni, that is our cue."

He kissed his mother and his wife, and smooched at little Lisbane's cheek, and the men set out the back door. David was the first to mention it, "So Gianni tells me you have Arabians..."

LADY JAYNE WENT THROUGH the entire 20 minutes of wedding planning with her jaw flapping about the services that would revolve around their wedding. All the pomp. All the circumstance. All the glitz, glamor, and puffery that came with marrying nobility, Vanity Devons threw out the window.

"That is not who we are," she said to her mother-in-law. "I live a very simple, uncomplicated, unglamorous life. Your plans would make me pull out my hair."

The stuttering started and each time Jayne tried to speak, she only stuttered more. "Allow me to explain, Lady Jayne. Those Hollywood movies aren't real, neither is that life."

"But you and Nigel were all over the news! You make the front page of almost every paper! He was even on the cover of several London gentlemen's periodicals. Social columns, world news! How could you not want to invite the world to such a spectacular, grand event?"

She held her hands as if she were about to pray as she pressed the tips of her index fingers to her lips, "It's sort of like this; the more reclusive and exclusive you are, the more people want. The rest is all smoke and mirrors. Half of those people at that event were called in by my assistant. I don't know them and I only have two friends. I don't surround myself with people. I don't have an entourage. And you met my personal staff."

Jane was a starting to understand. "So you and my son are a great deal alike then? Hard working, small social life, and very private."

Vanity was grinning from ear to ear which made Lisbane start grinning as well. "If we could, Lady Jayne, I would like the wedding to be small and intimate, with just close friends. Can we have it at Strathmore Keep?"

"Yes, it would be no problem. Is there anything special you would like?" she asked Vanity, almost worried about the success of the wedding.

"Actually, there is one thing that I would really like."

IT WAS A MILD NOVEMBER in comparison to other years where every fireplace in Strathmore Manor would be blazing, but this year was calmer. After showing David and Chuck around the manor, outbuildings, stores, and barn, Nigel bragged about Gianni and the ideas he had given him about making the country estate greener. The last thing he wanted to share with the men was the gym. It was state-of-the art with combination machines, a Jacuzzi, and a sauna.

Always a good judge of character, he knew this is where Chuck would want to stay for a while. Gianni was happy to make use of the Jacuzzi and Nigel asked David to come with him. As they entered the kitchen, Babette was preparing Vanity's next meal and nearly sliced off her finger as David passed close by her. Alarmed, he stopped to check her finger and the woman nearly swooned. He spoke to her in French as he swaddled her finger in a kitchen cloth, cautioning her to use ice to tamp the swelling down.

Nigel seemed disgusted by the whole show. Both of his wife's brothers were ridiculously handsome, smart and talented. "And how many languages do you speak, Mate?"

"Last time I counted, I think I was up to six," David said as he followed him down the narrow staircase.

"Six, really?"

"Yes, I mean Portuguese is the language our mother taught us first, then French, and English, and I also speak Mandarin, Cantonese and Chinese."

Nigel had stopped in the stairwell, looking up at David asking, "Really?" David only nodded.

"And Wilhelmina?" Nigel wanted to know.

He rolled his eyes upwards, "Portuguese of course, French, English and Italian, oh yeah and basic Spanish." David stopped, "Where are we going, Nigel?"

He waggled his brows at David, "I want to share something with you that I know you will appreciate." At the base of the stairwell, deep under the estate, Nigel opened a creaky wooden door and turned on the lights. David inhaled sharply.

There were rows and rows of nothing but wines. There were oak barrels of cognacs that David ran his fingers across, asking "Are these made by a la bonne chauffe distillation?"

"Actually they are. How did you know that?"

David was looking at the logo, "I had the pleasure of tasting some of this about five years ago and have been trying to get my hands on a bottle of it ever since."

Nigel walked over to the shelf and pulled out a bottle, "Here you go."

David's eyes got wide. "Do you know how much this is worth?" He stopped himself. Of course, Nigel knew how much it cost. He took two glasses from an enclosed case and rinsed them in the sink, drying each with a soft cotton towel.

"I very rarely get to share my collection with a fellow wine lover who truly appreciates the taste of the grape, versus those people who only want to collect the bottles." He looked around the cellar. "Well, I collect as well, but I also enjoy what I have. Please allow me the honor of sharing something with you."

David watched with interest as Nigel went to the back shelf and pulled out a bottle of red wine. He showed David the label and he gasped.

"Nigel, are you really going to open that?"

"Yes, and we are going to drink it as well."

David swallowed hard as Nigel sank the corkscrew into the top of the bottle and pulled up the cork on the 1925 Biondi Santi Brunello di Montalcino Riserva. It was easily a $25,000 bottle of wine, but David wasn't going to turn it down. Nigel allowed the wine to breathe as he went back to the shelf and pulled four more bottles of wine and placed them on the counter. He poured them both a glass, "Cheers!"

David's hands were trembling as he brought the glass up and swirled the contents before bringing it to his nose to inhale the bouquet. Last, he turned the glass up to his lips, allowing the vintage nectar to roll over his tongue. There was no way he was going to swirl and spit this out. Riserva was produced from Greppo's Sangiovese vineyards and was made only in exceptionally good years. Every bottle sold was at least 25 years old. It was everything David had expected and more. It was so good, he turned his back to Nigel.

"It is so good, I have to turn around so you don't see my raging boner," David said as he continued to drink the wine.

"Bloody hell, Mate, then don't turn around because you will surely see mine," Nigel said with a chuckle.

There were two large chairs and each took a seat. "We will serve the rest with dinner tonight."

David asked, "Are you serious?"

In Nigel's mind there was a cause to celebrate. His wife had told everyone she wanted to start a family. Two people were required had to have sex to do that! Which in Nigel's mind meant she was preparing to have sex with him. It wasn't the wine that aroused him, but the idea that soon, he would consummate his marriage.

The glass in David's hand was held tightly. "I'm afraid to drink it all, it is so delicious. How many more bottles do you have of this?" David knew he was going to throw out some astronomical number.

"Three. I had five in all. The one we opened and the one I gave you, which leaves me three," he said as he inhaled the bouquet again. "Have you looked at the bottles I placed next to your chair?"

David picked up the first bottle and tried to read the label, but he couldn't. He looked at Nigel, who was still sitting there inhaling the bouquet of his wine. The second bottle was a Bordeaux that had a crusted label with a "T" and the

Roman numeral 8. Bottle three was a French wine that was extremely old in a thick glass bottle. And the last bottle, he could barely tell what it was because of the dust. David looked at Nigel again. "I don't understand Nigel, these are extremely old."

"Wilhelmina said you recently bought a vineyard and were a neophyte collector. She also said you were studying to be a Sommelier. I am gifting you with these four bottles for your collection," he said.

"I am embarrassed that I can't read the labels. I don't know what it is you have given me," David said.

Nigel leaned forward in the chair, "The French ones came from Napoleon's personal stash after the French Revolution and the ones with the "T" came from the cellars of Strathmore Keep. They belonged to Henry the Eighth."

David was overcome with gratitude and didn't quite know what to say. Words came to him as he spoke softly, "And you are entrusting me with something so rare, so delicate, and so precious? These wines are beyond value. They are irreplaceable," David told him, feeling honored and humbled at the same time.

"Now, you understand how I feel," which is all Nigel had to add.

{29} Places please...

The evening had become still as Nigel stood in front of the fireplace, a glass of cognac in his hand and his wife on his mind. The more he sipped at the fine libation, the deeper he delved into thoughts of her. He imagined the feel of her long legs about his back, the sound of her passion as he brought her pleasure, and fantasized about how it would feel to be inside of her. He was so far gone in his thoughts, he did not hear her walk up on him.

"Nigel, you are deep in thought. What's on your mind?"

He did not face her but still stared into the fire. He spoke the words softly, only for her ears, "Vanity's Pleasure."

"Is there any reason why you are thinking about my business," she asked him.

His eyes came up slowly to meet hers, the passion seated deep in his irises, "No. Not your business."

He watched her cheeks flush.

Still blushing, she asked, "I just came to see if you wanted me to play for you tonight?"

"No." His answer was so quick that she jumped. Without turning around, he said loudly, "May I have a moment alone with Lady Wilhelmina please?"

There was no hesitation as her brother, cousin, Gianni, and even Conall rose and left the room, closing the door as they left the master study. Calmly, he sat the glass on the mantle and pulled her into his arms. He held her, pressing himself so close that it was difficult to tell where his body ended and hers began. When his lips found hers, the passionate kiss took her breath away and his right hand pulled her even closer while his left hand slid down to her buttocks. His fingers pressed into the flesh, kneading, pressing, pulling, and needing. Nigel's lips traveled to her jawline, her neck, and he nibbled on her collarbone.

He remembered the term she used on the plane; hungry. "I am hungry Wilhelmina, so hungry," his lips found hers again. He hefted her up in his arms, wrapping her legs about his waist as he pressed her back against the wall.

"I am being as patient as I can, but Darling, I can't seem to find the right tempo," he moved against her, trying to tamp down the grumbling in his soul. His lips found hers again and he knew that if he didn't stop now, he wouldn't.

Slowly, he lowered her legs to the floor. "I am sorry. I have been in my cups."

His finger stroked the side of her face. Nigel's words were gentle like a soft caress as he spoke. He said, "If you were to play tonight, I could not promise you that if you came at me, I would be honorable."

"Nigel," Vanity replied softly.

"It's okay. I'll come to bed later or sleep down here," he said, turning his back to her.

"I can try to be with you tonight, if you're patient with me," she said, touching his sleeve.

"No!" He turned back to her and pulled her back into his arms, kissing her forehead, "I said I would wait until you are ready."

He released her, offering in parting, "Goodnight, Lady Wilhelmina."

She put her foot down. He wasn't going to do this with her brother and family in the house. It was her turn to raise her voice slightly, "Oh no, you don't! You pour that crap out of you a cup, go wash your face, and bring your butt to our bed. I will not have the staff gossiping that we are having difficulties after only weeks of marriage."

Nigel's eyebrows went up as the facial expression she made. She was angry and if she didn't look so extremely adorable, he would be almost put out by her tone. However, his wife was not done with him.

Vanity spoke through gritted teeth, "I am stressed beyond belief. Your mother made an unexpected visit and Lady Jayne is trying to recreate or outdo William and Kate's wedding. The cost alone had my mind spinning. My brother made a surprise visit. Lisbane has attached herself to me and I have to be in Milan in two days. My face is scarred and I nearly broke my butt yesterday when I got thrown from that horse. I have bruises all down my right side. So, don't you dare have three drinks and relegate your penis as your designated spokesperson."

The look of shock on his face was almost audible as she poked him in the chest with her finger. The lady continued to speak, with her hands resting on the hips he loved to hold. Vanity said, "Get your butt up to that shower and I will rub it, tug on it, even kiss it if I have to until you feel better and get some relief; now move!"

Nigel put the glass down and moved slowly towards the stairs. Vanity continued her tirade, "Why are you dragging your feet now? A minute ago you were dying of starvation! Get your hungry arse up the stairs to our room!"

As he gradually climbed the stairwell, he looked back over his shoulder, "Rub it. Tug on it?"

Vanity made a fist with her right hand, shaking it as if she were playing a hand of rock, paper, and scissors. To make it worse, she swatted him on the ass. In truth, she was more turned on than he was, but afraid to let him know. At least this way, they both would have somewhat of a happy ending.

EXPERIENCE HAD TAUGHT Vanity Devons to travel with everything she needed for her show. The plane was gradually loaded and the next two days whizzed by in a blur. Lisbane came back every morning to obtain a new dress, but after the second day, she sent Connall to pick her up. She left every evening in the tattered frocks she arrived in, so Vanity would not offend the girl's parents. Vanity was careful to make sure the little one earned the dresses and items made for her small body. Lisbane's tasks of keeping the floors clean and she swept up lace, picked up pins, and stuck needles in red pin cushions were the merits which earned her new clothing.

Everything seemed to be going to plan until a major roadblock was encountered. David was on the phone scheduling models, but unfortunately one of the male models had contracted food poisoning the day before the show. Vanity eyed Gianni, who looked over his shoulder to see why his aunt was staring at him.

Gianna had found his way back into the kitchen for more of Biddie's pie, asking, with a mouthful of pastry, "What? What is that look for?"

It was a pinch, and he would have to do. Conall was at least six feet tall and had a posture about him that worked as well. She was taking him, too.

"Conall, get over here please," she asked. As the young boy moved forward, Clarke took out his measuring tape and began to call out sizes that Jessica plugged into her tablet.

He too was like Gianni, wondering, "What are we doing M'Lady?"

"You are going to have to help me out, I hope that's okay," she said, jotting down notes before the departure.

Final alterations and designs were made and she was off to Milan. Giles was invited to show as well to see the modeling debut of his nephew. Nigel insisted that everyone stay at his Villa and he would join them the tomorrow. David, shocked by the size of the villa and even more so to find his sister knew her way around, knew the Italian staff and seemed right at home. He began to wonder how much time had Nigel and his sister spent together before he came to America?

The night before the show, she sat alone in front of the fireplace, sipping on a cup of hot cocoa. She heard the clearing of a throat and turned to see David standing there.

"Mind if I join you, Vain One?"

"Sure, have a seat. I want to say thank you for being here. You as a new father, on the road with me. I know Halley can't be happy about this," she told her brother as she touched his arm.

He was quiet and she knew what that meant. It was a delicate subject he wanted to broach. "Mina, I still own half the company and I was just concerned I guess with your limited experience and Nigel being a worldly man." David wanted to make sure he had not fed her to a wolf in noble clothing.

She should have been embarrassed but she and David had shared so much. So many intimate details and times in her life, especially when there was no one to turn to but him, but this was different.

Vanity loved him with everything in her, and trusted him with so much more. However, she'd finally reached a state of independence where she didn't need her big brother to hold her hand. She was a married woman. Speaking softly, she said, "I appreciate your concern, but my husband is exactly who you think he is."

He threw up his hands, "I didn't mean to overstep. I mean, I got married, then Will. I was just worried that you got married as well so you wouldn't be alone."

"I am never alone," she told him and smiled as she remembered saying the same thing to her husband, who was now walking towards them. She pointed, "See."

She rose from the lounger to greet him with a warm and affectionate kiss. "I missed you," she told Nigel.

"And I was counting the minutes to getting here," he said as he held her close. Now it was Vanity's turn.

"David, you're going to be a great dad," she told him.

"Really, you think so Mina?" He asked as she reached for her husband.

"I know it to be true," she said as her brother walked away, finally feeling confident that he could completely step out of her daily life.

THE MORNING OF THE fashion show, Vanity took an extra 30 minutes with her yoga routine. Clarke was seated, enjoying a chai tea and going over notes while Jessica was on her tablet, making arrangements for a detail that couldn't be overlooked. Vanity was joined by David, Gianni, and Chuck in the living room as they maneuvered through stretches, poses, and positions that Nigel thought were not humanly possible; especially for a man.

He almost envied the closeness his wife had with her family. His sister Catherine, he only saw on formal occasions where their mother demanded her presence. Arthur, his brother, lived in an adversarial relationship which there was just no getting around. As straight and narrow as Nigel lived his life, Arthur did the complete opposite. Fast cars, fast women, and fast money. When Nigel refused to bankroll his lifestyle, he stopped speaking to Nigel other than pelting him with snarky comments. He often referred to Nigel behind his back as Mr. Bean, which is why he tried to take off Chuck's head. But watching them this morning, her family treated him more like a sibling than his own.

He belonged to someone.

I belong to her.

If only I can keep up with her.

Keeping up was the hardest thing to do when Vanity Devons was at work. Nigel attempted to go backstage the evening of the event, but was unprepared to see so many scantily clad, if not naked, men and women. Vanity was cool as a cucumber in the middle of the fray. Clarke was a champ at keeping everything organized as everyone huddled up in a circle for prayer that was led by David.

"Nigel, take my hand," Vanity said, slipping her fingers inside of her husband's strong hand.

After the prayer David spoke to the group, "Let's make them want to buy everything you have on guys! Let's give them a great show! Places please!"

Nigel was ushered into the seating area next to the runway and David plopped down next to him. He almost could not process all of the sensuous designs created by his wife as he watched the beautiful bolts of silk he had sold her come out in beautiful lingerie that she named the Strathmore Collection. Cameras flashed everywhere and all eyes were glued to the runway. He tried not to seem prideful as Conall made his way down the runway in silk loungers and an open pajama top. A glance at Giles found the very rigid man, wiping away a tear of pride for his young nephew. The ladies in the audience hooted as a shirtless Gianni made his way down the runway in silk boxers and silk evening slippers.

The collection was small and the show only lasted a good 30 minutes as Vanity's collection was sandwiched in between two larger designers. The last catwalk run featured of all the models, and the designer made her entrance down the 80-foot catwalk. Dressed in red silk lady boxers, high heeled pink sandals with straps that came up to her knees, a pink lace camisole, and pugilist styled robe, Vanity Devons hit the runway. Her trademark hair billowed in the artificial wind that Clark was creating in front of the stage. She hit the pivot, thrust a hip at Nigel, and gave him a wink. Nigel began to rise up out of the chair as if he were going to follow her down the stage, but David and Giles both pulled at the back of his jacket, "Down, boy."

Nigel, moon-eyed, grinned at David, "Wife, pretty, love the pretty lady..."

"That's good, Your Grace," David said as he patted his brother in law on the shoulder.

Backstage was chaos as Nigel tried to make his way over to her, but he could never get close enough. She was surrounded by well-wishers, lovers of her work, and his friend Sir Roddy with a bouquet of daisies. Gianni was running interference, keeping many of the male well-wishers from getting too close. Vanity held up her hand and all the commotion stopped. She held her hand out to him and Nigel was given a clear path to stand at her side. The cameras flashed as he stepped into the fracas. He remembered his training from Clarke: right foot out, left side. Hand over hers. Don't cover the rings.

Jessica and Clarke were hard at work. David brokered deals for the new orders for boutiques and stores. Gianni covered rounding up models and issuing checks. Even Conall was assigned a task of getting all of the garments back on the racks for Clarke. Then he noticed that even his butler, Giles in the middle of the fracas. He wasn't sure what his butler was helping with, and Nigel felt out of sorts.

Then a lone thought surfaced as he asked himself, if any room for him existed in this world of hers?

He started to slide away from all the lights and glam until Vanity Devons pulled him by the arm back to her side.

"Yes, those silks came from Strathmore Textiles. Here, speak with my husband, Nigel Strathmore," she said, giving him a slight shove forward. And simple as that, he was in the midst of the fray. She had pulled him into her world and made him a part of the process. Nigel passed out business cards, took orders with his phone, and answered questions about the fabrics, all the while trying to keep up.

"No these silks are exclusive to only Vanity's Pleasure. But I have others not in this line," he told one aggressive buyer.

Nigel was fitting right in. It was her turn to make some adjustments to be a part of his everyday life.

Vanity Devons had a plan.

{30} Tell me again...

At the villa, Vanity went to the master suite, still wearing the hair and makeup from the show. Normally, Clarke would have stripped her down to Wilhelmina, but she needed to know. She entered their chambers still in character, dropping the robe to the floor.

Nigel watched her curiously, "You are still in costume Darling. Are you going to wash your hair tonight? I can help if you tell me how."

He wasn't in love with Vanity Devons. Joy filled her from head to toe with the realization that Nigel didn't want to make love to the character she played for the cameras. Nigel Strathmore wanted Wilhelmina Devonshire.

"Sure, come help me wash my hair," she told him as she unstrapped the first heel, then the next, tossing a shoe at him as she made her way to the shower. Agile fingers tested the water before she climbed inside, joined by him.

"What did Clarke put in your hair, it is stiff as a brick," he remarked, allowing the water to cascade through the tresses.

Her eyes wandered down his torso, then back up at him.

"So are you," she said as her hand reached for him. He winked at her. Gentle fingers surrounded him as she whispered, "I'd like to try Nigel."

The words were so soft that he thought he misheard her. He continued lathering her hair, using the detachable head to rinse away the stiff mousse and gels. He focused on the task of rinsing away the gook from her hair and not her words.

"Did you hear me, Nigel?"

He continued rinsing, "Yes. I heard you."

The water continued running as she stood before him. He added conditioner to the longs strands, soaking them through to the waist.

When he felt he'd found his voice, he asked, "Wilhelmina, how long has it been since you've made love."

"Seven," she said.

Nigel's voice rose several octaves. "Seven what, months, weeks," he asked thinking surely his wife didn't mean years.

She whispered softly, "Years."

Nigel dropped the shower head.

"I told you I wasn't good at it. And the two times I tried it was painful and awful, and humiliating," she said lowering her head.

He bent over to grab the shower head. Standing at his full height, Nigel continued to rinse her hair. Wanting to ask the question, but certain how to phrase, it, but he inhaled deeply, not wanting to hurt her feelings.

Nigel asked, "Wilhelmina, are you telling me that you are a virgin?"

Her face was scrunched as she looked at him. Her long hair still soaked in conditioner as she faced him, she batted her lashes, trying not to choke on the truth she rarely spoke.

"Technically no. Officially, kind of, I mean, well, you know," she mumbled.

"No, I don't know," Nigel replied.

"He wasn't very big, so I don't know if he was in far enough to actually, you know," she said with her head lowered.

Nigel burst into laughter. His wife, a rare bird and genuine good spirit, had a sense of humor. He touched her cheek, smiling at her.

"Well, we won't have that problem," Nigel offered with a great deal of assurance.

Her hand touched his chest as she grabbed for the large sponge and began to lather him up. Nigel watched her hands work as she found the courage to speak the words she needed him to hear.

"Nigel, I do want to try, but if I can't go through with it the first time, will you try with me again?"

He took the soapy sponge from her, "I will try everything I know to make you comfortable so that you can enjoy our intimate times together."

He gave her a wry grin, "I will make certain that Vanity receives her pleasure."

"Oh, Nigel," she threw her arms around him his neck, pressing her body close to his as he lifted her into his arms, pressing her back against the shower walls. He pressed the tip of himself into her but there was no give. She required time. Tonight, he would introduce her to something new.

As he turned off the taps, he carried her from the shower as they hastily dried themselves and made their way to the bed. Tonight he only used his mouth to introduce her to more pleasure as she cried out his name in the darkness of the bedroom.

It is a start.

The next morning she was on her plane and headed back to New York. He didn't want to let her go, but she needed to get back to the office. After the show came the work and she had so much to get done.

VANITY SAT AT HER DESK in New York, pondering over the sales figures from Milan. It was a good show with nice profits. In her overnight bag was one of the dresses she had made for Lisbane and she was toying with an idea. Lisbane Strathmore. Liz Strathmore. Lizzie Strathmore. All would be great brand name for children's clothing.

She was having trouble focusing. Her mind kept going back to her intimate evening with Nigel. Who would have thought that is what all the fuss was about? However, her husband wasn't amused when it came time for her to reciprocate and she declined with the excuse.

"No way Spiderman, you aren't going to drown me!" She sat at her desk lost in the thoughts of the little girl who had wondered into her life. Nigel passing out kisses to little Lisbane during tea and fighting with Chuck. He'd also given David several bottles of rare wine, in which her brother couldn't stop chattering about. Her husband.

Nigel. Nigel. Nigel.

As if he heard her call his name her phone rang. The clear, crisp British accent came through the line. "Hello Darling, are you missing me?"

"Terribly. I was just thinking about the last time I saw you. I know it has only been a week, but it feels like forever."

"It's almost quitting time on your end. Are you ready to call it a day?"

"I am, but for some reason, going upstairs to an empty bed doesn't sound that appealing. I wish you were here," she mused.

"Where in New York or in your bed?"

She swirled in her chair, going back and forth. "Both, actually. I think I might be getting a bit hungry," she replied blushing at the words.

The line went quiet and then her phone chimed. It was an IM with a photo of Nigel. Then another. And another. That one showed the man taking off his shoes.

Followed by his pants.

Then his shirt.

The next one he was turning back the bed covers and Vanity stared at the picture on the nightstand. She also noted the colors in the room realizing...

"No way!" She dropped everything and took off running toward her private elevator. "Have a great night, guys!"

Clarke only smacked his lips, "Uhmm, her stuff must be upstairs or something. Or Mr. Duchy is doing some sexy video chatting."

Vanity reached her upstairs apartment and made a beeline the bedroom. She opened the door to find a trail of daisy petals from the door entrance all the way to her side of the bed. On his side of the bed was her husband. Undressed and wearing a naughty smile.

"I wasn't sure if I should have made the petals to the piano to get you to play first," Nigel said.

She silenced him by jumping on the bed and rolling across him planting his face with kisses, "I missed you so much."

"And I you," he held her but pushed her back a bit. "I am here because I want and need to talk to you."

"Is everything okay Nigel?"

For the next seven minutes, and she timed it, she listened to him speak about how much he loved her. Nigel spoke of his fear that she would bore of him and their life together and leave him for some Hollywood type with a cleft in his chin.

"I am scared that I love you too much and you are going to break my heart," he confessed.

It was her turn to speak.

"Oh stop being daft!" she said to him.

His eyes were wide as her dismissal of his genuine fears. He'd traveled across the pond to come and see her to express his concerns and she called him daft. In a word, his feelings were hurt.

Her fingers ran up and down his arm as she spoke to him. Vanity confessed, "I have been playing the piano since I was five years old and it has never turned me on in that way. What turned me on was playing the piano and having you watch me play. Hell, being in the same room with you turns me on. Watching you sleep. Eat, drink cognac, and even when you walk in the room, my hormones go haywire."

She straddled him on the bed.

"I have been hesitant to give myself to you out of fear that it would just be another conquest and once the fantasy was over, you wouldn't want me anymore," she told him.

Vanity also told him, "Greta Garbo once said, 'The story of my life is about back entrances, side doors, secret elevators and other ways of getting in and out of places so that people won't bother me."

She leaned forward and kissed him, "That is my actual life Nigel and I am so sick of it."

He moved a strand of hair that had come loose as she was running like a mad woman to get to him.

He wanted to know, "So what do you propose we do wife?"

"I want you to know that I love you so much that it scares me as well. I am all in. I want it all. I want it all with you. Yes, I know I have to make concessions and let some things go, but I can't see flying back and forth."

"Tell me what is next, Wilhelmina, tell me what you need me to do to make us right," he said as his mouth found hers.

"I need you to join us together Nigel and give me your son so that we can be a family and Conall will have a job," She told him, trying to return his kisses.

"I can do that," he murmured as his mouth found hers and he rolled her to her back. His kisses deepened as his fingers roamed her body, yanking at the skirt she wore, pulling it down over her hips. Patience Nigel, he cautioned himself. Take it slow Nigel, this isn't a race. In the back of his head were her words that both times had been painful and awful. He could feel the tension in her arms and legs as he positioned himself.

"Relax Darling, we have time. I will take it slow," he said as he felt her relax.

"Nigel, are you going to fit. I mean, is it going to be painful?"

His fingers touched her gently.

"No, it is going to beautiful. We are taking the first step to creating our son. I promise to make it good for you," Nigel assured his wife.

Vanity got weepy-eyed. "I'm going to be a great mom, Nigel."

"I know, Darling, but right now, I need you to be a great wife, help me out a bit, okay love," he said as he moved over her. His hands, his mouth were everywhere. Her body was on fire as she felt him move lower in the bed to use his mouth like he had before she left last week. She liked this part. His tongue flicking, adding moisture, tasting, testing, touching her core.

"Oh my, Nigel, that feels... ooh," she said as she felt his finger penetrate her delicate folds while his tongue worked some more. She moved against his hand, feeling the wonderful sensation building inside of her. The fingers of magic continued as his head came to her breast, taking a nipple into his mouth. Vanity bucked against his hand.

"Oh Silk!" She murmured into his shoulder.

The sensation stopped as he removed his fingers and placed his hands on her hips gripping them tightly, his mouth went to hers connecting them in a passionate kiss as he thrust forward connecting them at last. There was no warning. No attempts at a gentle entry. Vanity threw back her head as she tried to catch her breath.

"Oh, Shirttails, that hurts," she said, closing her eyes, squinting through the pain.

"Give it a moment," he gritted out through clenched teeth. The tightness surrounding him took all of his discipline to focus and not turn into a friendly, neighborhood, web slinger.

Nigel withdrew and pressed into her again. Harder this time and deeper. This time it didn't hurt, but felt different. Freeing. Liberating. The sensations of pleasure rippling through her as she found the words coming from her mouth was less than lady like and she didn't care.

"Oh Shit that feels good Nigel. Again! Do that shit again and harder!"

He withdrew and slammed back into her again, going deeper. Vanity cooed. The perfectly manicured nails scraped across his back as she rolled her hips upwards to meet his next thrust, and the lunge after that one, as she begged him for more. Nigel's fingers dug into the flesh of her hips as he raised them and planted himself all the way inside of her.

"Oh hell, yeah, Your Grace," Vanity yelled into his ear.

Nigel began to perform a series of long strokes, followed by short strokes, until he was covered in a fine sheen of sweat. Vanity had started to see stars, unicorns and puffs of cotton candy floating in the air.

"More, Nigel. More, Baby, give me some more of that," she encouraged him as he pulled back and plunged deep, forcing her climax.

Vanity grabbed him by his hair, stared him in the eyes, and yelled a string of obscenities that were so loud and raunchy that Nigel stopped moving and looked at her. His face was full of concerns as he looked down on the timid woman who barely uttered a swear word but had developed the language of a drunken sailor.

"Did I hurt you, Wilhelmina?"

She was clinging to him, not letting go, shuddering through her climax. Trying to catch her breath she spoke in a husky tone while licking dry lips.

"Yes. No. That shit feels so good. I came so hard I see spots," she told him as she moved with him. "Your turn Nigel, come inside of me and give me our son."

He kissed her again, "I love you so much, Wilhelmina." His movements became faster, his pace quickened, his breathing labored, and he prodded hard, breathy, anxious, excited, and rigidly he drove into her softness. He wanted to give everything he had inside of him to his wife. Nigel pumped harder. Gripping her hips, holding her still as he prepared to give her his seed.

"Wilhelmina," he called her name as he charged hard again and again shuddering in the beauty of the release. Finally, he'd connected with his wife on an intimate level. Finally, making love to her as he wanted to for the past months. Finally, consummating his marriage. Nigel collapsed on top of her, spent.

Quietly, they lay in the bed holding on to each other, but Nigel was the first to speak.

"That was some language there, M'Lady. I thought you said no self-respecting woman used those kinds of words," he said through a chuckle.

She pinched him playfully on the arm.

"I think you just shagged the respect out of me," she laughed, covering her face with the bed sheet. "I am so embarrassed. I won't make a habit of it, but M'Lord, that was fantastic."

Her eyes had started to tear up and she began to cry.

"Wilhelmina, are you in pain Darling? Please tell me I wasn't too rough with you," Nigel said.

Through her tears of joy she told him no, their lovemaking had been perfect. Her phone rang and the ring tone was her twin brother.

"I'm sorry, I have to get this," she said to Nigel reaching for the phone.

"Uhmm, hello," she said through her sniffles.

Will was on the other end. His voice was laced with concern for his twin. Anxious words rushed from his mouth.

"Willie, are you okay? Is everything all right? I was just hit with this huge wave of emotions and now I feel like I want to cry. Are you crying?"

"Yes, I am crying, Will."

"What's wrong Willie, talk to me," Will coaxed.

She was quiet as her fingers ran through the hairs on Nigel's chest, "I'm okay. Nigel and I, uhm, we just made our son, I think."

"Ew! Shut up. Just shut up. Oh, yuck," Will exclaimed and with that, her brother hung up.

Vanity looked at Nigel. She found herself giggling again, as she wrapped loving arms around his waist. Snuggling close, she held onto her husband, planting a kiss on his chest.

"See, it was so good even my brother felt it," Vanity said.

Nigel kissed her again. "Tell me again Wilhelmina. Tell me once more," Nigel said, burying his nose into the top of the mass of hair.

"That shit was good! You are the official Guv'Nah of Happy Town!" She laughed loudly.

"Not that you silly goose, tell me again, about how much you love me," Nigel said.

"Oh Nigel, this is how love feels," she said in a high pitched girly voice as she batted her eyelashes at him.

She wrapped her arms around his neck, "I love you, Nigel Strathmore."

"I love you too, Wilhelmina."

{31} All in the family...

It is said that if you want to make God laugh, tell him about your plans. In Vanity Devons' mind, God was having quite the row, because everything in her world changed in one night. Her plans to become a mother happened far faster than she had anticipated, along with several other life-changing events.

On the outskirts of Glastonbury, a loud boom was heard three nights before Christmas, waking everyone within a three-mile radius. The fire brigade responded, but much of the sleepy hamlet had to be evacuated as the fumes from the crystal meth lab took over took the streets, filling it with poisonous gases.

Vanity's heart sank when she heard of the death of Lisbane's parents as she and Nigel donned protective masks, searching through the aftermath of the rubble for the child. After about an hour, devastated and in tears, she was surprised when Nigel's phone rang and Giles informed him that the child had been found upstairs in Strathmore Manor in the guest room, asleep.

When told of her parent's demise, Lisbane's only question was, "Lady Wilhelmina, will you be my Mum now?"

She cradled the child to her chest, crying with joy that she had not been hurt. Nigel turned his head to hide his emotions as his wife. After obtaining his consent and a bit of paperwork, Vanity Devons became a mother to Lisbane. A month later, she found out she was soon to be a mother in her own rights. A child that made her eat everything, including the scraps in the kitchen sink. No matter how much she ate, she never seemed to be full and spent every day constantly seeking something upon which to graze.

This kept Babette busy. Between the nightly battles with Lisbane for a bath and keeping her Lady fed, the poor girl was dead on her feet. Nigel rewarded her with a hefty bonus for consenting to care for Lisbane, which pleased the girl to no end. He even tacked on an additional week to her annual holiday plans.

Nigel, too, was pleased. Lady Wilhelmina was glowing and had spent the last month at his side in England. Jessica was running the New York office, but he knew something was off with his wife. On a quiet Tuesday morning, she came into his office at the London factory, her eyes welling with tears.

"It's done," she told him as she flung herself into his arms.

"Wilhelmina, Darling, what has happened," he implored as he sat her upon his lap.

"I sold it," she cried as her body shook from the force of her tears.

Nigel was confused, "Sold what, Darling? Talk to me."

She sniffled, wiped her nose on the back of her hand, and yelled in his face amidst a blubber of tears, "I sold Vanity's Pleasure!"

And she balled louder. He hadn't asked her to do such a thing and based on the revenue the company generated, it was a very lucrative business. It still perplexed him to no end that a woman could pay that much for a pair of lacy knickers, but they did.

"If David forced you to sell it, I will look at having a rod with him," Nigel said, rubbing her back.

It took a minute for her to regain her composure and he allowed her time.

"No I sold it because if I didn't I would never grow. If I didn't sell the business, David would always feel as if he had to be at my side during shows instead of with his family, which is where he is needed. I have to start a new chapter," Vanity said through soft snobs.

Yes, Nigel was very confused. He had not asked her to give up her company or what she loved doing most. He held her as her tears subsided.

"It's time to do something new. I sold the company and I am starting two children's lines of clothing. One called Tiddly Twins and the other Liz B. Strathmore," she told him.

Nigel's sat in awe of her. The children's market was even more lucrative than lacy knickers, and she would easily make a small fortune. However, he was uncertain why the change all of a sudden.

"The Liz B Line will be high end, with exclusive one-of-a-kind clothing for the clients who don't want their kids wearing off the rack and the other is made just for the rack," she said.

She pulled out a picture of David's twins, Trey and Amanda, showing him a photo of the boy and the girl in coordinating outfits, which were close, but not identical.

"I got the idea when I saw many of the old photos of Will and me. Our clothing was always a sore spot for me, which is why I started designing clothes in my spare time. The clothing line will grow with the twins," she said.

She used her tablet and thumbed through the designs.

"These are absolutely genius," he told her as he stopped on a photo of Lisbane in a cute frock with a matching hat. "I really like these. Is this that hideous pattern of fabric that was in the back of my closet?"

She smiled as she thumbed through a few more images.

"It is so ugly, it is cute," Nigel said.

Vanity showed him several more outfits using that fabric and another bolt that he could not sell to any clothiers and he could not help but laugh.

"I could do exclusive lines with the bolts that you cannot sell," she told him.

Nigel couldn't take his eyes off the fabric that was too ugly to even made bed pillow, yet she'd transformed it into a marvelous product. He had questions about how she planned to proceed after she closed out the old lines.

He asked, "Darling, how did David feel about being put out of a job?"

"He was fussing until I handed him his half of the check. Then all of a sudden, he thought it was the greatest idea ever," she said through a sniffle.

Nigel rubbed her thigh. "I am still confused as to what prompted you to do this. I know what VP meant to you," he said looking at her.

She gazed into his eyes. The news she actually came to tell him she offered with no emotion in her voice.

Vanity said, "I can't continue to run that size of a business with two small children raise."

Nigel was looking back at her. As with his conversation with her twin, it took a moment for the spoken words which traveled through his ears to reach his brain.

"Lisbane is not that big of a handful and Babette is there to help," Nigel said and stopped. "Wait, what do you mean by two?"

Vanity smiled at him as she touched her stomach, "You are about to be a dad. Again."

"I don't know if I can handle this," he told her with a smile. "I have been married for five months and I am a father of a five-year-old hellion who is obsessed with pink and a baby on the way."

"Yes, but Collingswood will give her a run for her money," she told him with a wink. Nigel stood up so fast he dumped her off his lap. "How long have you known? When did you find out?"

Vanity picked herself up off the floor, dusting off her bum. "I found out last week. I am only 6 weeks along, but, I think it's a boy. I am hoping it's a boy," she replied.

He helped her get to her feet.

"You are having a boy? I mean we are having a girl? Holy Silk Balls!" He ran into the factory, losing all of his regal composure and bearing. "We are having a baby thingy!"

The machines were silenced as the staff looked up and he yelled at them again, "I am pregnant! We are having a baby." A few snickers resounded as she stood next to him. The workers new in his excitement and understood that she was carrying the next heir to the Strathmore line. Wilhelmina only prayed that it was a son.

She also prayed that she could fit into her wedding dress.

AS THE DAYS SPED BY and April looming around the corner, there were many details to be completed. The wedding dress Vanity had initially purchased for her ceremony had to be scrapped and she made a new one that fit around her growing belly so the pregnancy was not so obvious. Her parents, who had arrived in March, immediately noticed the pudginess.

Nigel quickly brought his hand up to his nose, "We are already married! Don't hit me!"

Elena was a ball of nerves and each time she looked at Vanity, she would start to cry in her elation for her daughter. This upset Vanity because each time her mother cried, she cried too, which upset Clarke who could not contain the puffiness around Vanity's eyes. Finally, irritated beyond measure with all of the crying, the swearing from Clarke, and Lisbane crying each time Vanity cried, Nigel called his mother and sent Elena to assist Lady Jayne with the wedding details.

"I am certain you have a great deal to catch up on since you last saw each other," Nigel told her as he loaded Elena into the Bentley and sent her to the Keep. It greatly mellowed out the rest of the week.

Each time Will looked at his sister's belly and at Nigel standing next to her, he would frown and say, "Ewww!"

Elsie was too far along in her pregnancy to travel to England, and Will was going to try to catch it all on film.

Gianni's only comment was, "Cool, 008 is growing in the pod."

He looked about the kitchen for Biddie, "ooh, is there pie?"

David had arrived with Halley and the twins, whom Vanity immediately fell in love with. She had not seen them in person since their birth and had only interacted with them via video chats. They were so adorable that she could not help but cry.

This made Lisbane cry.

This made Clarke start cursing.

Which made Lisbane mimic him and Nigel sent Clarke to the Keep to help the mothers. A day later they sent him back. Elena's only words were, "He is too disruptive."

Disruptive was a mild way of putting the words chaotic maelstrom. Clarke was convinced the headless ghost of Anne Boleyn was chasing him through the castle trying to make him straight. He claimed the ghost slipped into his room last night and tried to handle him under the covers.

The ever composed Giles' draw dropped, his face contorted and he frowned when he asked, "What?"

The attention now focused on Clarke, who took to center stage, retelling his story to a captive audience.

"It was horrible. A headless naked ghost chasing me around, all ghostly and stuff, booing at me, saying oooooooh, take me. I tell you all, I was truly afraid for my life, child. I was screaming at that sheer ghost lady, Girl! Where you wanna go?"

The expression on Giles face made David Sr. lose it. He fell over on the couch, holding his stomach in gut busting laughter. But the butler could not wrap his mind around what Clarke was inferring.

Giles asked, with his nose turned up in the air, "Are you implying that you were chased by a headless ghost who wanted to copulate with you?"

"That's what I am saying Jeeves!" Clarke remarked with

"The name is Giles," he told Clarke.

"Whatever your name is, I was scared just that bad. I can't even think straight. A queen needs a drink," Clarke said.

He sashayed out of the room followed by Lisbane who was mocking the way that he walked, tagging along behind him, her hand on her tiny hip.

"And a princess is going to get some milk," Lisbane added.

Cookie, who had been very quiet the entire trip, looked at her uncle and asked, "Uncle David, can I go back to my kitchen? These people are confusing me."

David Sr. had laughed himself so hard, that he had rolled off the couch on to the floor lying on his back like a dead cockroach. He looked at Giles, who was standing in the corner, a deadpan look on his face as he watched the two saunter off. This only made David Sr. laugh harder.

"Bloody hell! I don't know if I am going to be able to survive all of this," Nigel said as he sat in a slump in his chair by the large hearth. David had brought with him a special bottle of wine that he had been saving and poured him a glass.

"Welcome to marriage and my crazy ass family, Your Grace," he said as they both swirled, inhaled and sipped.

Two days later, a large family dinner was planned. During dinner, with everyone gathered and Jessica and Clarke at the table, Vanity presented them her new idea and new company plans. She looked to Khalea to help her get it set up. Her gaze went to Jessica.

"I don't know if I can do it without you. I would love for you to help me build this," Vanity said softly.

The girl was quiet, but Nigel spoke up.

"I have something for you Jessica," he said before handing her an envelope. "It is a 30 day trip through South America starting April 20th. You will be assigned a travel companion to accompany you and it is all expenses paid."

Jessica, overwhelmed by Nigel's generosity began to cry. This made Vanity cry. And of course Lisbane's lip begin to quiver. And for some odd reason, Clarke started to tear up as well.

Nigel stood up.

"Please, please, please, for the sake of all that is sacred! No more tears ladies," Nigel said as his gazed wandered over to Clarke. David Sr startled chuckling. Although he uttered the command, it did little good when he told Jessica that if she decided to accept the job offer, there was a small cottage on the property that she could move into. "We can have it all ready for you to move in when you get back from South America. I mean, if you want the job."

He never gave her an opportunity to answer because he moved on to Clarke.

"There is also another cottage on the property as well, if you want it Clarke," he said with a bit of a terse face.

"Oh hell naw! I am far too beautiful to be squirreled away like some country mouse. I am a city queen, and a queen needs her drones to worship her," Clarke said aloud.

David Sr started choking.

Gianni looked about the room, "Do we have any more of that pie?"

But Nigel wasn't done. "I'm glad you said that Clarke. I could really use some help to rebrand some of my lines. I want to do a couple of catalogs and some advertising for some of the older fabrics, you know branch out. I could really use your expertise."

Clarke clutched at his green pearls, "that's fine, but it must come with a flat in the city, 'cause I am not living out here. You don't even have street lights. It's creepy as hell. I looked over at the woods, and I swear I saw some yellow eyes looking back at me." He crossed himself and said something in Spanish. "I was hoping you were sending me to Abu Dhabi, but I guess employment is just as good. The Abu Dhabi mens gone have to wait."

And he poked out his lip.

Giles was still standing in the corner just staring at Clarke with a blank face. David Sr lost it again. Wiping away the tears of laughter, he looked at Giles, who had not moved from his spot, or changed his blank expression as Clarke rose to grab the bottle of wine from the center of the table and turn it up, guzzling it. David Sr laughed harder.

Nigel extended his hand for a shake to Clarke, "well, here is to a very interesting beginning to something I am not certain of what I am doing."

He looked at Gianni, "However, something I am certain of, is you young chap." He handed his nephew in law an envelope. "This is my initial investment in your future and your consultation fee for the time you spent helping me make this manor greener."

Gianni was at a loss of words when he looked at the check. But Nigel wasn't done, "I have an internship here for you next summer if you want it."

"I sure do!" He grinned at his Dad. "If it is okay Pops?"

Will looked at his sister's rounding belly, then back at Nigel, turning down his mouth at the sheer thought of how the two of them made a baby. His only reply was a wave of his hand and say, "eeww!"

It was good enough for Nigel.

"Raise your glasses," Nigel said. "To new chapters!"

{32} Here comes the brides...

The wedding day started with a beautiful morning at the manor, and Will finally having the chance to ride one of the Arabians that David and Gianni bragged so much about. As her brothers mounted up and Gianni mounted the Walera, Nigel had one of the Shire ponies brought out for Chuck.

"I figured this would be more your speed, Mate," Nigel said with a wry grin.

Chuck didn't find the humor in the joke and his rants at Nigel were missed as Vanity walked out of the Manor, in a soft pink silk robe, her hair down, and both billowing in the April morning wind. Nigel's breath caught at the sight of her as he turned his horse and galloped towards the house.

He brought the horse to a high stepping trot before it lowered its head to greet Lady Wilhelmina. Nigel reached down from the mount, sweeping her into his arms and seating her upon his lap as he took a slow trot around the back garden while he kissed her thoroughly and then deposited his lady on the back doorstep. She presented him with a silk scarf that he tied around his neck before galloping back up the hill to join her brothers for an early morning ride.

Will was frowning, but David only nudged his younger brother.

"You have to give it to him, that was rather romantic," David said.

Will, still frowning, replied, "Yeah, it was. Well, he did promise to sweep her off her feet in grand fashion."

Nigel joined the group, a full-blown grin on his face, "Let's ride Mates!"

He took point as the group galloped over the hill. The morning ride was short. Showers, change of clothing and the need to have the entire family bussed over to the Keep for the wedding ceremony.

The wedding took place that afternoon, quietly, with little to no fanfare as Nigel and Vanity committed themselves to one another a second time. David Sr. was happy as he raised his daughter's veil and kissed her cheek before once more, placing her hand in Nigel's. Vanity's brothers along with Arthur, Sir Roddy and Sir Thomas served as Nigel's groomsmen. Halley, Jaelon, Khalea, Cookie and Phan served the bridesmaids to Lady Wilhelmina.

Everything almost went without a hitch until Lisbane started to throw a tantrum during the end of the ceremony. Nigel gave her a stern look but it was not enough to get her under control. The pretty pink frock she wore was about to be ruined as she made an attempt to throw her little body to the ground in a tantrum. Babette tried to carry her out, but she turned her little frame into a dead weight until Vanity had to stop the ceremony to address the child who was adamant that Nigel should marry her as well.

Lisbane protested, "I am part of the family too! He should marry me too!"

Vanity shrugged her shoulders as she motioned to Giles, who brought up a chair for the child to stand in. Nigel's eyes were wide in disbelief.

"Are you bloody kidding me, Wilhelmina?"

Nigel pointed his finger at Lisbane, who had stopped crying as she held Wilhelmina's hand. Her large blue eyes stared at him with love and adoration. A large grin upon her little face, showing off where she had lost a tooth. When the minister pronounced them man and wife, instructing Nigel that he may kiss the bride, Lisbane puckered up for her kiss as well. Nigel looked at the audience that began to clap as he bent to kiss her little lips.

Lisbane faced the small crowd and yelled, "Yeah! We are married!"

"Well, you can never say you will be bored as my husband," she told him as he took her in his arms.

"I have not had a dull moment since I met you," he said, as he lowered his head to kiss his wife, but his kiss was halted by the blowing of a horn.

A tractor trailer pulled up to the front of the Keep and rolled its way into the courtyard. Everyone was shocked at the interruption of the ceremony as the driver climbed down and began to unhook his cargo.

"Bloody Hell! What is the meaning of this blatant intrusion?" Nigel wanted to know.

"I have a delivery here for the Guv'Nah of Happytown, Nigel Strathmore eye vee. My instructions were to get it here before 3 pm. It is 2:56 and I got it here."

Nigel corrected the driver, squinting his eyes.

"That is the Roman numeral four. Not the letters I and V," Nigel said.

He also turned slowly to look at his wife, who seemed delighted at her jab at him. When the driver opened the rear door and lowered the gift, Nigel's jaw dropped. From the back of the trailer rolled out a 2019 Silver Cadillac CTS with mag rims with a gigantic bow on it.

The Duke was all smiles as he looked at his wife.

"A modern piece of American beautiful," he said with a grin.

Vanity stood at his side, "I bet you say that to all the girls."

"No, only to my wife."

LADY JAYNE SAUNTERED slowly along the tables of food and walked upon David Sr. who turned and bowed over her hand, "Your Grace," he said with his deep baritone. Even at nearly seventy years old, he was still a very dashing figure of a man with serious eyes and a toothy grin.

"Your children are absolutely wonderful people," she told him. "I feel so blessed having your daughter as part of our family."

"It does my old heart good to hear you say that Lady Jayne," he said as he sipped at the glass of champagne, but he knew better. She wanted something. Never one to mince words he asked, "So, what would you like to know?"

"I want to know all of it," she said as she placed her arm in his to guide him towards the family room.

"What do you mean?" He asked in all seriousness.

"I mean, my friend Elena was going to America to study music and her father was the newly appointed ambassador of Portugal. Then I heard she had run off with some black man and had gotten married and her father left the US in a scandal. So, I am asking, because she will not discuss it, what happened?"

David Sr grinned as he watched his wife sit down behind the Blüthner to play a song for the reception. All of these years later, she still had not lost her touch on the ivories. Today, she was equally as beautiful as she'd been years ago, during the height of the civil rights movement. He a young attorney freshly appointed in Washington, D.C. with a clientele only the history books would annotate upon his death. They were in love and willing to risk it all.

"I want to say it was a simple as two people falling in love during one of the most turbulent times in American history, but it was so much more than that. Because as you well know, that when Elena decides she wants something..."

-Fin-

Discussion Questions?

1. How many times have you been surprised when people have believed you to be one way and learn you were someone totally different?

2. Sometimes, as women, we have difficulty communicating our sexual needs to our partners. Did you understand Vanity's fear?

3. We each have a public persona and private persona. Vanity was concerned that Nigel was in love with her public image. How did the two differ?

4. Nigel was patient as he taught his wife to trust him. Did you feel he gave her enough time?

5. Did you finally understand David's relationship with his sister?

6. David Sr was not pleased with Nigel. Discuss some of the matters in which he took exception to a foreigner and why.

7. There were several large changes in Vanity throughout the course of the book. Discuss your favorite moment as her character came to terms with her new life.

How about some holiday cheer?

Santa's Big Helper, Available December 24, 2014

ABOUT THE AUTHOR

O livia is a USA Today Best Selling and multiple award-winning author who loves a good laugh coupled with some steam, mixed in with a man and woman finding their way past the words of "I love you." An author of contemporary romances, she writes heartwarming stories of blossoming relationships about couples not only falling in love but building a life after the sensual love scene.

2015 Swirl Award Winner, Best Erotic Romance, Thursdays in Savannah.

2017 IRAE Award Winner, Best Contemporary Romance, Wyoming Nights

2019 IRAE Award Winner, Favorite Series, The Men of Endurance

2019 IRAE Award Winner, Reader's Choice Award

2019 Nominee, Top Female Authors, The AuthorShow.com

When Olivia is not writing, she enjoys quilting, playing Scrabble online against other word lovers and spending time with her family. She is an avid world traveler who writes many of the locations into her stories. Most of the time she can be found sitting quietly with pen and paper plotting more adventures in love.

Olivia lives in Hephzibah, Georgia with her husband, son, grandson and snotty evil cat, Katness Evermean.

Learn more about her books, upcoming releases and join her bibliophile nation at www.ogaines.com[1]

Subscribe to her email list at http://eepurl.com/OulYf[2]

Facebook: https://www.facebook.com/olivia.gaines.31

Twitter: https://twitter.com/oliviagaines[3]

Instagram: https://www.instagram.com/gaines.olivia/[4]

1.   http://www.ogaines.com/?fbclid=IwAR2FnGurgSPr_a5iEgjJJRaZTBWUhl7EZYSa0kf8i5OoRohd-NU7f4NWh44s

2.   https://l.facebook.com/l.php?u=http%3A%2F%2Feepurl.com%2FOulYf%3Ffbclid%3DI-wAR1jIyQAJ5Xj6cV1l09Q3S4MKJ85ZvoN_HA5Xdel-bURrmq2L9t9pAogp0k&h=AT3EKRi6GxY-bL22a_I1EEnWDPplT1Qxa6F49_RAWZdQNayh0EiHHlSGxRhT0_Ayl9T4IR7_yHj_GVTfjrqb-htquIPw4XUMqOQQgSFIsXVmUjvgPcyYgXKRtiGu2eZJ2o6PyceNS_hv0p5m-GqFTuIA

3.   https://twitter.com/oliviagaines?fbclid=IwAR3URbr7aM8f3fk0FkEFOzJHrwbi-Uwg6VkHQZKvGmQFnO3TAOfwiyLVnGEM

4.   https://www.instagram.com/gaines.olivia/?fbclid=IwAR0ZkThCUVBlCRfSK8usRTTmoFe-qX_fv_UNrPE66a8uvS7QlrmSidOvLu14

Don't miss out!

Visit the website below and you can sign up to receive emails whenever Olivia Gaines publishes a new book. There's no charge and no obligation.

https://books2read.com/r/B-A-KVAB-MCFZ

BOOKS 2 READ

Connecting independent readers to independent writers.

Did you love *Vanity's Pleasure*? Then you should read *Killers*[5] by Olivia Gaines!

Yunior Delgado has been inadvertently taken by a group of human traffickers who don't know who they have. One phone call to Saxton Blakemore and the wheels are placed in motion for the daring rescue.

In the wee hours of the morning, four technicians load up to collect the heir apparent, with telling results. The fixer, the tracker, and the retrieval agent are joined by a blast from both the past of Saxton and Mr. Yield.

The story deepens as Yunior begins to understand the man he is supposed to be, versus the man he believes walks in his shoes. At the end of the day, surrounded by Killers, his role as the impending Czar of the Americas unfolds incrementally as he tries on the loafers which are a perfect fit.

Read more at ogaines.com.

---

5. https://books2read.com/u/boWgKa

6. https://books2read.com/u/boWgKa